Trapped in Paradise

"I'm sure you already know this, but I have to tell you, your home is beautiful," Paige said, walking along the periphery of the library, taking in the leather-bound titles as Micah followed closely behind.

"And I'm sure you already know this, but so are you," Micah said. "It was so important to me that you love this place as much as I do," he continued quietly. "But I knew. I knew the moment you saw it that you had fallen in love."

A warm rush raced over Paige's skin as he moved his hands to her waist. She looked up at him, her eyelids heavy. "How could I not?" she said. "It's . . . fascinating."

As they gazed into each other's eyes, Paige felt the same dizzying sensation she'd experienced at the restaurant the night before, but it was okay. She was beginning to enjoy it—this feeling of being lost in his eyes.

"You haven't even seen the best part yet," Micah said, his voice throaty.

"The best part?" she repeated, temporarily incapable of forming her own thoughts.

"The garden," Micah said, his eyes flashing with excitement. "You have to see the garden."

More titles in the

Pocket Books series

THE POWER OF THREE

KISS OF DARKNESS

THE CRIMSON SPELL

WHISPERS FROM THE PAST

VOODOO MOON

HAUNTED BY DESIRE

BEWARE WHAT YOU WISH

CHARMED AGAIN

SPIRIT OF THE WOLF

DATE WITH DEATH

GARDEN OF EVIL

All Pocket Books are available by post from:
Simon & Schuster Cash Sales. PO Box 29
Douglas, Isle of Man IM99 1BQ
Credit cards accepted.
Please telephone 01624 836000
fax 01624 670923
Internet http://www.bookpost.co.uk
or email: bookshop@enterprise.net for details

GARDEN OF EVIL

An original novel by Emma Harrison

Based on the hit TV series created by

Constance M. Burge

POCKET
BOOKS

LONDON • SYDNEY • NEW YORK • TOKYO • SINGAPORE • TORONTO

First published in Great Britain in 2002 by Pocket Books.
An imprint of Simon & Schuster UK Ltd.

POCKET
BOOKS Africa House, 64–78 Kingsway, London WC2B 6AH

Originally published in 2002 by Simon Pulse,
an imprint of Simon & Schuster Children's Vivision, New York

POCKET BOOKS and colophon are registered trademarks of Simon & Schuster.
A CIP catalogue record for this book is available from the British Library

ISBN 07434 61010

3 5 7 9 10 8 6 4 2

Printed and Bound by Cox & Wyman Ltd, Reading, Berkshire

*For Matt . . . for always
listening to my ramblings*

Chapter

1

The warm afternoon sun tickled the back of Paige Matthews's neck as she rolled over onto her stomach and flattened out the pages of the glossy entertainment magazine she was reading for the fifth time. It was a cloudless spring day in San Francisco, and the beauty of the great outdoors had lured Paige, her two sisters, Phoebe and Piper Halliwell, and their significant others, Cole and Leo, to Delores Park—along with the rest of the neighborhood. As Paige pulled her dark sunglasses over her eyes and looked around, a group of squealing children ran by playing tag and a pair of lovers walked hand in hand through the green grass, whispering sweet nothings to each other.

It was all enough to nearly drive Paige insane. She lifted her head to look at Phoebe and Cole. "Hey, do you guys want to—"

Paige cut herself off the moment she saw what they were doing. Cole was dangling a whipped cream–dipped strawberry over her sister's open mouth, and Phoebe's head was tipped back to accept the fruit. Her long brown curls tumbled over her shoulders and down to the blue picnic blanket. They may as well have been posing for the cover of one of Phoebe's favorite bad romance novels.

"Never mind," Paige said, rolling her big blue eyes as Phoebe giggled and bit into the strawberry.

"Uh . . . you guys?" Piper said from the other side of the blanket, glaring at the sickeningly sweet lovers. "I thought we were going to try to be a little more . . . uncouply this afternoon." The fact that her own love interest—her husband, Leo—had wandered off momentarily seemed to designate her leader of the non-couple campaign.

All three of them looked over at Paige, their faces clouded with guilt. Paige felt an embarrassed, irritated blush creep over her otherwise milky white complexion.

"Don't lose the goo factor on my account," she said, sitting up straight and slapping her magazine closed. She reached up and tightened her ponytail, going for nonchalant. "Just because I haven't had a boyfriend in months, and there are absolutely zero prospects in my immediate future, doesn't mean you have to tiptoe around me."

"No. Piper's right," Phoebe said with a little

nod, moving a couple of inches away from Cole and rolling her shoulders back resolutely. "We don't have to be all over each other all the time."

"Speak for yourself," Cole said, taking a flirtatious nibble at Phoebe's neck.

"Cole!" Phoebe shrieked, laughing as she swatted him away. "Down, boy."

"I'm sorry!" Cole said, his teasing pout totally incongruous with his usual dark and brooding demeanor. "If the bounty hunters are going to leave me alone for five minutes, I'd like to use those five minutes to their full advantage."

"Hey! Nibble away!" Paige said, waving her hands at them. "Cole's right. Some freakish minion of the underworld could appear at any moment to hunt him down and you might not see him for days."

Paige opened her magazine again and forced herself to stare at it. But she couldn't concentrate on a single word on the colorful page in front of her. Instead, she attempted to mentally deal with the fact that her conversations now included phrases like "minions of the underworld" and "bounty hunters."

It wasn't that long ago that Paige was just a normal, only child, going through her day-to-day life as a social worker, blissfully ignorant to the otherworldy evil lurking all around her. But ever since Phoebe and Piper had entered her life, she'd been learning new and freakish things every day.

First of all, while Paige had always known she was adopted, she'd been shocked to learn that her real mother—also Piper and Phoebe's mother—had been a witch. Not only that, but her father had been a Whitelighter—a supernatural force of good who protects witches. With parents like these, it was clear to all three sisters that Paige should have some serious powers. It hadn't taken long for her to find out that she could not only orb—make herself disappear and reappear in a whole other locale— but that she could also orb objects from one place to another.

Paige was a powerful witch—one of the Charmed Ones—and when she was together with her sisters, they could pretty much conquer anything: demons, warlocks . . .

Anything except a serious romance drought.

"There you are!" Piper said suddenly, shaking Paige out of her thoughts. She knew from the sweet giddiness in her sister's voice that Piper was welcoming her husband, Leo, also a Whitelighter, back to the picnic blanket.

"For you, fair maiden," Leo said. He handed Piper a huge bouquet of wildflowers, and Piper's face lit up before she caught herself.

"Thanks, honey! You brought flowers for . . . all of us!" Piper said brightly. Clearing her throat, she quickly split up the bouquet and gave a third of the flowers to Paige and another big chunk to Phoebe. "Wasn't that nice of Leo?"

Piper asked, pushing her straight brown hair behind her ears.

"Nice try, Piper," Paige said, gazing down at her flowers.

"Okay. What'd I do?" Leo asked tentatively, raising his eyebrows as he sat down next to Piper.

"Nothing," Paige told him with a quick smile. "They're just trying to get my mind off my extreme lack of boyfriend. And failing miserably."

"Oh," Leo said, his face creasing with an apologetic frown. "Anything I can do? I mean, besides kind-of bring you flowers?"

"Yeah. Know any nice Whitelighters you can set me up with?" Paige asked, squirming up to sit on her knees.

Leo shot Piper a wary look and she glanced away, scratching behind her neck—a telltale sign that she wanted to avoid the question.

"Well—"

"Come on, guys!" Paige said, biting her bottom lip. "Where else am I going to find a guy who understands my new superhero lifestyle?"

"You don't want to go there, Paige. Trust me," Piper said, busying herself with opening Tupperware boxes and ripping apart a package of napkins, causing them to fly all over the place. Paige raised her eyebrows at her sister's sudden manic mood swing.

"Piper and I went through a *lot* to be

together," Leo explained, reaching out a hand and stopping Piper's arm before she could cause any more destruction. "The Powers That Be did almost everything to keep us from getting married. I wouldn't wish that experience on anyone. Especially not you."

"Fine," Paige said with a sigh.

Normally she found Leo's monster protective side endearing, but at that moment she could have done with a little less big brother and a little more matchmaker. Unfortunately, it was clear that wasn't going to happen, so instead she turned to her next best bet to cheer her up: sweets. She dug into the picnic basket in search of some chocolate-covered pretzels.

Fruit . . . crackers . . . cheese . . . .

"Uh . . . Piper?" Paige said, sitting back from the basket again. "Did you get my pretzels?"

Piper winced and slapped her hand to her forehead. "I'm sorry! I completely forgot," she said. "But I made cookies."

She held out the Tupperware box as a peace offering, and Paige peeked inside. It was filled with little butter type cookies with some kind of fruit substance in the middle of each one. *Fruit.* So *not the point of cookies.*

"Thanks, anyway," Paige said, feeling irrationally disappointed. What was the big deal? So what if Piper had forgotten the *one* thing she'd asked her to get? The girl was busy, what with running her club, P3, and fighting evil all the time. *Still, it wouldn't have been that hard for her to remember one little thing. . . .*

"Hey, Paige, come on," Phoebe said, pushing herself up to her feet and straightening her shirt. She reached out her hand to Paige. "Let's go snag some ice cream from the cute ice-cream-truck boy."

Paige laughed. "What, you think the ice-cream-truck guy is the one for me?" she asked.

"Well, if he *is* you can get your sugar fix *and* a date at the same time," Phoebe said with a grin. "How efficient is that?"

Paige rolled her eyes again, but she took Phoebe's hand and let her sister pull her to her feet. Who knew? Maybe the ice-cream-truck guy *was* her destiny. And if not, at least she knew there was a swirl cone out there with her name on it.

Phoebe Halliwell was feeling quite content as she and Paige walked arm-in-arm across the park. While she was dedicated to the calling of the Charmed Ones, she savored these rare days when there was no evil to fight, when there were no glory-grubbing demons after her boyfriend, when she could just enjoy a tranquil day in the park with her family.

"So, we've all been annoying you with our gushiness lately, huh?" Phoebe asked, scrunching her nose as she looked at her sister.

"Well, it's kinda hard not to feel lonely when

you're living with two perfect couples," Paige replied as she kicked at a long patch of grass. "Don't get me wrong—I'm glad you guys are so happy. I just wish I could be happy, too."

Phoebe smiled sympathetically at Paige. There was a time not so long ago when she'd felt just like her little sister. And it wasn't until she'd stopped focusing so much on dating and had gone back to school that she'd happened to meet Cole.

Of course, once she'd fallen in love with him, she'd found out he was a half-demon who'd been sent to do away with her and her sisters. But Cole had since turned against his evil master and dedicated his life to doing good—thus the demon bounty hunters who were out for his blood. Apparently the bad guys didn't take well to traitors.

"You're going to find someone," Phoebe assured Paige, shaking her long hair back from her face as a breeze whipped by. "These things always happen when you least expect it."

At that moment, a flash of color went whizzing by Phoebe's face and she let out a little yell, raising her arms to protect herself. When she whirled around to see what had attacked, she had to laugh. A bright red Frisbee was lying a few feet away from her in the grass.

"Jumpy?" Paige asked with a smirk.

"I guess I'm just skeptical about a danger-free day," Phoebe said, shaking her head at herself.

She glanced across the field and saw a pretty

African-American girl a couple of years younger than Paige jogging toward them. Phoebe picked up the Frisbee to throw it back to her, but she froze before she could even lift her arm.

The vision hit her with a blinding force and she squeezed her eyes shut, clutching the Frisbee in one hand. She saw the girl who'd missed the catch, screaming at the top of her lungs, as a hideous creature with razor-sharp, six-inch-long claws advanced on her. The girl cowered against a cluttered desk, terrified as she tried to fight off the demon, but in about five seconds, the creature had torn her to shreds.

"Phoebe? Are you all right?" Paige's voice cut through the vision as it slowly started to fade.

Phoebe realized that her sister was supporting her from behind, and was absently grateful she hadn't had this particular vision while she was on her own. If she had, she'd be sprawled out on the ground right now. Paige yanked the Frisbee out of Phoebe's hand and Phoebe struggled to regain control over her breathing.

"What did you see?" Paige asked.

But Phoebe couldn't answer her yet.

That was so real, I felt like it was happening to me, Phoebe thought, clutching Paige's forearm. Her visions were getting more and more vivid by the day, and sometimes she could barely stand to recall them—like when they featured innocents getting mauled for no apparent reason.

"Hey, thanks!" the Frisbee girl said, finally

catching up to them. "I'm kind of a spaz at this."
She took the Frisbee out of Paige's hand, apparently unaware of Phoebe's near-transparent
complexion.

"Find out who she is," Phoebe whispered to
Paige.

"Uh . . . hey! Don't I know you from somewhere?" Paige asked with a friendly smile. She
let go of Phoebe, who took a deep breath and
managed not to crumple to the ground.

The girl looked at Paige uncertainly. "Maybe.
I'm really bad with faces," she said. "Do you go
to San Francisco State?"

"Yeah! Yes," Paige lied, scrunching up her
face as if she was trying to remember something.
She stuffed her hands in the back pockets of her
jeans. "Were you in my . . . English class last
semester?"

"Creative Writing? Yeah!" the girl said with a
friendly smile. She reached out her hand to
Paige. "I'm Regina Trager."

"Right! Regina!" Paige said as she grasped
hands with the girl. "I'm Paige Matthews."

"It's nice to meet you," Regina said. "Well, I'd
better get back to my friends." She cast one last,
searching look at Paige and Phoebe before she
jogged over to a small group of chattering girls.

"Regina Trager," Phoebe repeated weakly. "I
bet that girl has no idea what she's in for."

Piper came running up next to her at that
moment and grabbed her hand, obviously having

noticed the fact that she'd almost keeled over.

"Hey, are you all right?" she asked, smoothing Phoebe's hair away from her face as she studied her.

"Yeah, I'm fine," Phoebe answered shakily. She wiped her sweaty palms on her skirt and sighed. "But we have to help that girl."

"What happened in your vision?" Paige asked, crossing her arms over her chest. "I thought you were going to go horizontal for a second there."

"Some demon," Phoebe answered, shuddering as she remembered the violence of what she'd seen. "Some big, scaly thing with Wolverine claws . . . " She trailed off, gazing at Regina as she ran after the Frisbee again.

"He doesn't . . . *kill* her, does he?" Paige asked, glancing over her shoulder as well.

"In a very not pretty way," Phoebe said with a nod.

Piper slipped her arms around Phoebe and gave her a comforting squeeze, and Phoebe smiled her thanks.

"Don't worry," Piper said. "We'll go home right now, find this thing in *The Book of Shadows*, and figure out how to vanquish it."

"Well, we'd better do it fast," Phoebe said. "Because if we don't get to Regina before that thing does, I really don't like her chances."

Chapter
2

By the time the sisters had returned to the Manor, Piper was feeling more than a little uneasy. Phoebe was still pale and shaken from her vision, and Piper knew that her sister was playing and replaying the awful movie over and over in her head so that she wouldn't forget a single detail. She hated that her sister had to go through that. Even though Phoebe's visions had helped the Charmed Ones save dozens of innocents and vanquish countless demons, Piper wished Phoebe didn't have to suffer through them so often.

"Phoebe, why don't you sit down for a minute?" Piper said as Phoebe started immediately up the stairs. "I'll make you some tea."

"Piper, we don't have time for tea," Phoebe said, her hand on the banister. "We have to find the vanquishing spell, track down Regina, and stake out her house. Tea is not an option."

"Okay, okay, you're right," Piper said reluctantly. "But as soon as we get a chance, you are taking a rest."

Piper followed Phoebe and Paige upstairs to the attic, where the girls kept *The Book of Shadows*. She still couldn't shake the nagging feeling that they were in for something particularly scary and wished Leo were here. But when the girls had announced that they were going to go home to do some digging, Leo had decided to talk to the Elders to see if they had any information and had orbed out pretty quickly. Piper admired Leo's dedication and respected the requirements of his all-important job, but it didn't make her miss him any less when she needed him.

I wonder how Phoebe does it, Piper thought, watching her sister as she rushed over to *The Book of Shadows* and started flipping through its thick, musty pages. *At least Leo isn't being pursued by demons-for-hire.* Cole had also disappeared when the sisters had decided to go home. It was always better for him to keep on the move when he could so that the bounty hunters couldn't get a lead on his location.

"Ah! Here he is!" Phoebe announced, jabbing her fingertip into the book.

"Ugh . . . that thing?" Paige asked. She leaned in toward the page, her face a mixture of disgust and disbelief. "Hello, Freddy Krueger."

Not much wanting to see their new nemesis after that description, Piper nevertheless approached her sisters. They stepped aside so she could look at the book and her heart pretty much plummeted to the floor. "'Aplacum,'" she read from the top of the page. "Well, he's not winning any demon beauty pageants."

The Aplacum was a huge, hulking creature with the physique of a giant football player. It was covered in scales and had seven fingers on each hand, each boasting a long, sharp talon. From the seething grimace on its creepy face, it hadn't seen many happy days.

"There isn't much information here," Piper said, flipping the page. "It doesn't say what it's after or why it kills or how."

"I think we know how," Paige said, swallowing hard.

"And it does have a vanquishing spell," Phoebe pointed out. "That's all that matters, right? We can kill it before it kills our innocent."

"Okay, I'll write this down. Paige, why don't you find out where this Regina Trager girl lives?" Piper suggested.

"I'm on it," Paige said. She turned on her heel and rushed out of the room.

Piper grabbed a pad and pen from the window seat behind her and started to copy out the vanquishing spell. There was a potion included, and she was careful to copy down the exact amounts of each ingredient. One wrong measurement and who knew what could happen? She might end up making the

Aplacum stronger instead of conquering it. Magic was tricky that way.

"Come on, Phoebe," Piper said, tearing off the sheet of paper when she was finished. "Let's get you that tea."

"Sounds like a plan," Phoebe said, tenderly bringing one hand to her temple.

Phoebe followed Piper out of the attic and down the stairs silently. They crossed the hall and descended the stairs to the living room. By the time Piper had arrived in the kitchen and a single word had yet to be said, she was worried about Phoebe all over again. Her little sister was nothing if not wordy. Piper filled the teapot with water, slapped it onto the stove, and turned the burner up to HIGH. Then she turned to Phoebe, one hand on her hip.

"Okay, what's wrong?" Piper asked. "You've never been this quiet before. We figured out how to vanquish the demon, so what else is bothering you?"

"Nothing," Phoebe said unconvincingly, slowly climbing onto one of the stools surrounding the island in the center of the kitchen.

"Why don't I believe you?" Piper asked.

"I don't know . . . I have this weird feeling that there was someone or . . . some*thing* else in the room in my vision," Phoebe said, crossing her arms on the island's tile surface in front of her. "Something else evil. Is that weird?"

"Did you *see* this something else?" Paige

asked, flouncing into the room with the phone book in her hands, her dark brown ponytail bouncing.

"No. It's really just a feeling," Phoebe said with a shrug. "An overall icky feeling."

"Well, maybe that's just because the vision was so violent," Paige said, sliding onto the stool next to her and flipping open the thick phone book. "It's probably just affected you more."

Piper looked at Phoebe hopefully. "Do you think that's it?" she asked as she reached up into the magic cabinet—the storage place for all ingredients of the magic persuasion. Piper, an expert chef, liked to keep her eye of newt as far away from her peppercorns as possible.

"Maybe," Phoebe answered uncertainly.

"I got her!" Paige announced, holding up the phone book with a grin. "She lives at one of the sorority houses on campus."

"Thank God she's listed," Phoebe said. "At least something's going right today."

"Everything's going right," Piper said, infusing her voice with confidence. She crouched down and pulled a few of her stainless-steel pots out of one of the cabinets. "We'll make up this potion and get our butts over there before Aplacum can attack. And I am going to make us a little extra protection, just in case your hunch is right about this added evil."

Piper stood up again and placed the pots on the free burners. She opened a drawer and pulled out three inch-long purple crystals, then she filled the smallest pot with bottled water from the refrigerator.

"This spell requires Poland Spring?" Phoebe asked, arching one eyebrow.

"The purer, the better," Piper said.

She turned on the burner and waited for the water to boil, then threw a few ingredients into the bubbling liquid and stirred it with a wooden spoon. When the mixture had turned a Pepto-Bismol–worthy pink, she tossed the crystals into the mixture, creating a puff of pink and white smoke. Satisfied, she drained the crystals out of the liquid into the sink and handed one to Phoebe, one to Paige, and kept one for herself.

"Cool," Paige said, holding the now snow-white crystal up and turning it around in the light. "What's it for?"

"Keep it with you tonight and it should protect you from any unexpected evil," Piper said, tucking her own crystal into her pocket.

"Wow. You've become like the Julia Child of the Wiccan world," Phoebe said, clearly impressed.

Piper blushed and lifted one shoulder. "I do what I can," she said as she started to slice and dice the ingredients for the Aplacum's vanquishing potion. She just hoped her sister was right about her talents in the kitchen. Because at the moment, it seemed Regina's life depended upon them.

• • •

"Do you think you could suck a little bit less loudly?" Piper asked, glancing at Paige in the rearview mirror of the SUV that night.

"Sorry," Paige said, rolling her eyes. She stuffed her lollipop into her mouth and let it rest in her cheek. "Maybe if you'd let me *drive*—"

"What does driving have to do with your lollipop?" Piper asked, rubbing at her forehead with one hand as if she were talking to the most frustrating kindergartner on the playground.

"I just don't understand why I can't drive your car every once in a while," Paige said. "Is it because I'm the youngest?"

"No. It's because you can't go to the post office without dinging it," Piper said.

Paige felt her face heat up with embarrassed indignation. "Hey, that mailbox came outta nowhere."

"I don't see what the problem is," Piper said, sounding exasperated. "You have your own car."

"Yeah, but it's a total clunker," Paige pointed out.

"Well, maybe there's a *reason* it's a clunker," Piper said.

"Girls! Can we not argue about this now?" Phoebe blurted. "Do I have to remind you why we're here?" She gave Paige and Piper each one of her rare serious glares, and Paige leaned back into her seat. She knew better than to press Phoebe when she was in a scolding mood. It hardly ever happened, so when it did, it was a pretty big deal.

Paige sighed and glanced at the windows of Regina's brightly lit sorority house. It was a sprawling, stucco structure that was surrounded by trees and colorful flowers—more like a resort than college housing. Paige and her sisters were staked out in the shadows across the street and they'd been sitting there with nothing to do for over an hour. Nothing except bicker, that is. Paige had rung the doorbell when they'd first arrived and had been told that Regina was out with her boyfriend. Since Phoebe had seen Regina attacked in what appeared to be her bedroom, the girls had decided that as long as the girl was out on a date, she was safe. In the meantime, they were keeping their eyes peeled for the Aplacum.

"I don't know how you can consume so much sugar, anyway," Piper said under her breath.

"Hey, you guys have men, I have candy," Paige shot back.

She saw Piper and Phoebe exchange a guilt-ridden glance, but she didn't care. At least she had gotten them to stop picking on her.

"What I don't get is why this Aplacum thingie wants to kill an innocent college girl," Paige said, pulling her lollipop out of her mouth as she watched a group of students stroll by loaded down with books. "Do you think she's a witch?"

"Who knows?" Phoebe said. "Maybe she just

has something the Aplacum wants."

"Like some serious moisturizer," Piper joked.

Paige laughed and caught Piper's eye in the mirror. Piper smiled, and Paige instantly felt better. She'd never had siblings until recently, and it still surprised her how easy it was to let go of grudges and arguments as if they had never happened. It was kind of cool, having sisters.

"Well, there are always those random demons who kill just for the fun of killing," Phoebe said, fiddling with the fringe on her long sweater. "I don't know about you guys, but I think those are the scariest kind."

There was a moment of silence as Paige and her sisters contemplated this, but it was broken by the sound of a car drawing near. Paige leaned forward in her seat and, sure enough, a little red convertible pulled up in front of Regina's house and killed its engine. Regina climbed out, laughing and blushing and looking generally giddy. She was followed by the single hottest guy Paige had ever seen.

"Wow," Paige said under her breath. "Regina sure knows how to pick 'em."

Regina's boyfriend was tall and slim with dark hair and eyes that were so blue, Paige could even *tell* they were blue in the dark from yards away. When he smiled at Regina and took her hand, Paige's heart actually skipped a beat. She'd never had that kind of reaction to someone's simple smile before. Certainly not when he was smiling at someone else. He was wearing a killer suit and carried himself like a person who knew exactly where he was going and what he was going to do when he got there. Paige caught herself on the verge of salivating and stuffed her lollipop back into her mouth.

"Well, *that's* not the demon," Piper said.

"We can't be so sure. Remember a certain guy named Cole?" Phoebe said, opening her car door as Regina and her man disappeared into the sorority house. "I think we should get a closer look."

"Why? For her protection or because you're in a Peeping Tom kinda mood?" Piper asked archly.

Still, she and Paige both climbed out of the car and quietly closed their doors behind them. They crept across the street and down the driveway. None of the front lights had gone on when Regina had gone inside, so they tiptoed around back. Sure enough, Regina and her boyfriend were clearly visible inside a bedroom on the first floor.

"That's it," Phoebe said under her breath as the girls ducked down. "That's the room I saw in my vision."

Paige swallowed back a surge of fear and raised herself up a bit for a closer look. Regina and her boyfriend were standing in the center of the room, laughing over something he'd said, and now that Paige could see the guy more clearly, she could tell that he was a few years older than Regina. He was definitely in his early to mid twenties and he definitely had some serious bank at his disposal. His suit was not only impeccable, but expensive, and his shoes shone like they'd never been broken in.

Suddenly, he caught Regina's face between his hands and leaned in for a long, tender kiss. Paige watched, seized with an irrational wave of jealousy. She knew she should look away and give the poor kids some privacy, but she couldn't. All she could do was wish that she were the one being kissed in there.

Then, in a flash of green and yellow light, the Aplacum suddenly appeared in the corner of Regina's bedroom. Paige's heart jumped into her throat. The demon was even more frightening in 3-D full color. It let out a tremendous roar, and the couple flew apart.

"Omigod, you guys," Paige said, reaching out a shaky hand and catching Piper's arm.

"Show time!" Phoebe said, jumping up. She leaped onto the back porch and kicked the door down, tearing it from its hinges just as Regina let out her first, earsplitting scream.

Paige and Piper ran up the steps and followed Phoebe into Regina's bedroom. Regina was pressed back against the desk, screaming and raising her arms in front of her face as the Aplacum advanced on her. The demon pulled back one of its monstrous hands, ready to strike. The sharp, silver talons glinted in the overhead light as it brought its arm down.

"Piper!" Phoebe shouted.

Piper lifted her hands and froze the room with the Aplacum's claws hovering just inches from Regina's face.

"That was close," Phoebe said, holding her hand over her heart.

"Okay, what do we do now?" Paige asked, glancing behind her at Regina's boyfriend, who had apparently been thrown to the floor before they had made it inside the house.

Piper pulled the little bottle of vanquishing potion she'd concocted that afternoon out of her pocket. "Phoebe, the second I unfreeze them, you're gonna have to distract the demon. Just don't let it get those claws anywhere near you."

Phoebe nodded and stepped up next to the frozen Regina, ready to fight.

"Paige, you grab Regina and the guy and get them out of the room," Piper continued. "It's too small in here for us to fight with so many people in the room. But get your butt back in here as quickly as possible. We'll need you for the spell."

"Got it," Paige said, nodding.

"Okay. Here goes nothing," Piper said. With a flick of her fingers, she unfroze the room, and the screaming started up again.

Phoebe jumped into action, kicking the Aplacum hard in what was most likely its stomach. It was kind of hard to tell, with its completely alien frame. The moment the thing fell back a few inches, Paige reached out and grabbed Regina's hand, pulling her away from the desk.

"You have to get out of here," Paige told her, clutching the girl's trembling shoulders.

Regina whirled around, hysterical, as Phoebe launched herself into the air and narrowly avoided getting sliced by the Aplacum. "Where's Micah?" she cried out.

"I'm here," Micah said, climbing up unsteadily. He looked into Paige's eyes and blinked as if he was suddenly taken aback. Even with everything going on around her, Paige felt a jolt of attraction and for a moment it was as if the rest of the room and all the madness in it faded to nothing. As beautiful as his eyes had been from afar, they were mesmerizing now. Then Micah tore his gaze away, and the trance was broken. Paige blinked, and he took one look around, seeming to come to his senses.

"Come on. Let's go," he said, grabbing Regina by the arm and pulling her out of the room, and Paige could hear him trying to wrangle a group of curious girls away from the door.

"I can't do this much longer!" Phoebe called out, ducking the Aplacum's swiping claws and sweeping its legs out from under it with one swift kick. Paige whirled around as the beast hit the ground, taking a lamp and half of Regina's desk with it.

"Piper, now!" Paige shouted.

Piper flung the bottle of potion at the ground,

where it shattered, sending a blast of purple steam into the air and obscuring the Aplacum from view. Phoebe leaped over the bed to stand next to Piper, and Paige rushed up to Piper's other side. Piper clutched the vanquishing spell in front of her so that they could all read in unison.

"Whispering winds, serve us well,
Take this demon back to Hell!"

The Aplacum let out one more mighty roar before it winked out in a blast of red light. A huge gust of wind burst from the floor and ripped across the room, tearing Paige's hair back from her face and ripping Regina's posters and photographs from the walls. But it was gone as quickly as it had come. The Aplacum had been vanquished.

"That wind was not exactly whispering," Piper said as she pulled a few Post-its out of her hair.

"Okay, do I still have all my fingers?" Phoebe asked, pressing her eyes closed and holding her hands out shakily.

Paige looked her sister over. "All ten digits present and accounted for," she said.

"Phew," Phoebe replied, opening her eyes with a grin. "Let's make a pact to never fight anything like *that* again."

There was a commotion in the hallway growing louder by the second, and Micah and Regina came bursting back into the room, clutching hands. Regina took one look around at her bedroom and then sat down shakily on top of a few egg crates by the door, clearly in shock.

"Everything's okay!" Micah shouted into the hall before slamming the door behind him.

"Is it really gone?" Regina asked, her voice quavering.

"Yeah. Don't worry. You won't be seeing that thing again," Phoebe said, reaching out and smoothing down Regina's hair.

The girl looked up at her and smiled gratefully through her tears. "What was it?" she asked, wide-eyed.

"We were kind of hoping you'd know," Piper said evenly. "You have no idea why it came after you?"

"I'm still waiting to wake up," Regina said, clearly baffled. "I've never seen anything like that outside of horror movies and nightmares . . . *which* I'm clearly going to be having tonight."

"Well, it's kinda hard to explain," Phoebe said, looking from Micah to Regina. "Let's just say we're witches and we fight bad things and we'd appreciate it if you didn't tell anyone about this."

"Witches?" Micah asked, looking at each of them. When his eyes fell on Paige, she felt her heart turn to goo in her chest, but she managed to shrug and crack a smile. Micah chuckled. "Well, whatever just happened here, we're really grateful for what you all did," he said. He crouched down on the floor next to Regina and took her hand. "I don't know how we would have survived if you hadn't been here."

"Yeah," Regina said, squeezing Micah's hand. "Thanks."

"There's no need to thank us," Piper said, stepping over the broken lamp as she headed for the door. She smiled down at Regina. "Try not to have nightmares. You're safe now."

"Sorry about your room," Paige said as Piper and Phoebe slipped through the door. Paige started to follow, but before she could, Micah looked up at her and she froze in her tracks. His steady, blue-eyed gaze was so full of unabashed attraction, she almost fell into his arms right there.

What are you thinking? He's just grateful, she chided herself, forcing her feet to keep moving. *Get over yourself.*

Still, she could practically feel his eyes on her as she headed out into the hall. Every inch of her skin was tingling with excitement. No guy had ever made Paige feel like that before. Not from a simple look. Was this what it meant to fall in love at first sight?

Chapter
3

"Good morning!" Piper greeted Phoebe brightly the following day. She stretched her arms above her head as she walked into the kitchen and took a long, deep breath. Piper was definitely a morning person. Especially on a beautiful, sunny morning following a night of demon fighting that had resulted in zero injuries and an incident-free vanquishing.

"Guess we didn't really need these," she said with a smile, tossing her protection crystal on the island in front of Phoebe, who was sipping coffee over an open newspaper. "Hey, I hope you saved the entertainment section for Paige. She'll be grumpy without her morning gossip fix."

Piper went over to the refrigerator and pulled out the glass jar of orange juice. It wasn't until she turned around again and got a good look at Phoebe that she realized something was up. As always, Phoebe was perfectly coifed and dressed in a pink shoulder-baring top and matching striped skirt, but she was staring off into space even though there was a fresh colorful Sunday style section lying in front of her.

"I see leg warmers are making a comeback," Piper said innocently, eyeing Phoebe for a horrified reaction. When she didn't get one, she slapped the jar of OJ down on the counter. "What planet are you on this morning?" she asked, waving her hand in front of Phoebe's face.

Phoebe blinked a few times and looked down at her flowered coffee cup as if it had just appeared in her hands.

"Sorry," she said, smiling in Piper's direction. She put the cup down and sighed, pushing her hands through her hair and causing her dozen sparkling bangle bracelets to clink together. "I'm just thinking about last night."

"And which part is throwing you: the dead demon or the totally grateful nonvictims?" Piper asked as she poured herself a tall glass of juice.

"Actually, it's that Micah guy," Phoebe said, rubbing her hands together in her lap as if she'd just gotten a chill. "I swear I've seen that guy somewhere before and it's been bugging me all night."

"Well . . . maybe you're just remembering him from your vision," Piper suggested. She pushed up the sleeves of her brown wool

sweater before she took a sip of her juice. "He
had to have been there, right?"

Phoebe narrowed her eyes as she thought it
over, then slowly shook her head. "I don't
know," she said, clearly frustrated. "I don't think
that's it. But even if that *is* it, isn't that a little
troublesome?"

"How so?" Piper asked, her brow wrinkling.

"Remember I said I thought there was some
other evil presence in my vision?" Phoebe said,
leaning forward in her seat. "What if Micah is
the evil presence?"

Piper sighed. She could tell her sister was
starting to get excited over the possibility of
being onto something, and she didn't want to
burst her sleuthing bubble, but this one was a bit
of a long shot. "Phoebe, come on—"

"No, Piper! What if Micah is some kind of
demon in disguise? Or even just a run-of-the-
mill dangerous criminal?" Phoebe said, growing
more and more vehement. "What if Regina is
still in some kind of trouble and we missed it?"

"Okay, you have to let this go," Piper said,
reaching out a hand and covering Phoebe's with
it. "Micah seemed like a perfectly nice guy. He
was just as shocked as Regina was over the
whole witches and demons thing."

Phoebe sighed and stared down at the tiled
surface of the island, looking almost disappointed.

"Besides, if Micah was bad, why wasn't he

the one hurting Regina in your vision?" Piper asked, lifting her juice glass to her lips.

"You're right," Phoebe said. She absently toyed with the edge of the newspaper, flicking the corner up and down with her finger. "We saved Regina. It's over."

"Right," Piper said firmly.

"Right," Phoebe repeated.

Piper, however, could tell that her sister's heart was not behind that statement. When something was bothering Phoebe it was next to impossible to get her to let it go with simple reasoning. She had to have solid proof or this Micah thing would nag on her forever. It was just one more of her sister's endearing—and sometimes irritating—qualities.

"So . . . that Aplacum thing was pretty creepy, huh?" Phoebe said with a half-smile.

"Yeah, I don't know about Regina, but *I* had nightmares," Piper said.

"I know. I barely slept," Phoebe added.

She sighed and reached for her coffee, but just as she was about to pick it up, the doorbell rang. Before Piper even realized what had happened, there was shattered ceramic all over the countertop and a huge coffee puddle was moving fast, about to spill over onto the floor.

"I got it! I got it!" Phoebe cried out, using a sheaf of newspaper to stop the flow.

Piper threw out her hands and froze the spill, then grabbed the role of paper towels from the dispenser over the sink and ran over with them. Together she and Phoebe mopped up the mess and threw the soggy newspaper and towels into the trash.

"A little jittery this morning?" Piper joked once the damage had been repaired.

"Insomnia," Phoebe said with a laugh. "Does it to me every time."

"I'll get it!" Paige called out when the door-bell rang for the second time.

She bounded down the steps and across the landing to the door, fully expecting to find a Girl Scout or some other door-to-door salesman type on the front step. She was trying to come up with a polite rejection—unless it was a cookie-bearing kid—when she swung the door open and her mind went entirely blank. Micah's blue eyes were smiling back at her. Paige immediately regretted going for the lazy-Sunday-in-sweats look.

"Hi," Micah said with that killer grin. "I hope I'm not disturbing you."

It took a second for Paige to find her voice and when she did, it came out as a bit of an unintelligible squeak. She laughed, flushing, and took a step back. "No! Not at all," she said finally. "Come on in."

"Thanks."

Micah stepped over the threshold, envelop-ing Paige in the musky, sweet scent of his cologne. She almost swooned. Her pulse was racing, and her palms were already slick with sweat. What was wrong with her? As Micah glanced around, quickly taking in the foyer, Paige checked out her reflection in the mirror next to the door and smoothed her hair down, her hand shaking.

"So . . . what brings you here?" Paige asked, smiling uncontrollably. Wow, he looked good. His shoulders looked particularly broad in the dark, lightweight coat he wore over yet another perfect suit, and the deep blue color of his shirt only made his eyes more mesmerizing.

Micah opened his mouth to answer, but before he could, Phoebe and Piper emerged from the kitchen and walked up behind him. Piper shot Paige a questioning glance, and Paige merely raised her shoulders, barely able to keep herself from giggling. She couldn't believe she was actually getting to see this guy again.

"Good morning," Micah said, turning to her sisters. "I was just telling your sister . . . I hope this isn't a bad time."

"No. We were just taking care of a major culinary mishap, but that's all cleaned up now," Phoebe joked, crossing her arms across her chest. "So, what're you doing here?" she asked bluntly.

"Phoebe!" Paige said through clenched teeth.

"What I think my sister means is, we're surprised to see you," Piper put in with a placating smile. "We didn't even tell you our names last night. How did you find us?"

Micah chuckled and looked down at his shoes. "I can see how that might throw you," he said, his blue eyes shining. "Actually, I recognized you from P3, Piper," he said. "I hang out there a lot and I knew you ran the place, so I called this friend of mine who works for you . . . Tyrell Brooks? He told me where to find you."

"Oh! You know Tyrell?" Piper said, her shoulders visibly relaxing. "He's a great guy. I'd be lost without him."

Paige raised her eyebrows, surprised. Tyrell Brooks was a guy in his early twenties who had worked his way up from busboy to assistant manager faster than even he had expected. He'd spent most of his young life in and out of shelters, on and off drugs, and skirting the law before he'd cleaned himself up. A few years ago, Piper had taken a chance and given him a job and he'd done nothing but impress her ever since. It wasn't that Tyrell wasn't well worth knowing; Paige was just impressed that a guy who drove a hot convertible and walked around in thousand-dollar suits would have a friend with such meager beginnings. Normally guys like Micah turned out to be snobs.

Piper reached out her hand. "So, it's nice to officially meet you, Micah . . . ?"

"Grant," Micah said, shaking hands with her. "Micah Grant."

"This is Phoebe, and that's Paige," Piper said.

Micah shook hands with Phoebe, and Paige held her breath as he turned to her. She quickly wiped her palm against the thigh of her sweatpants and clasped hands with him. The moment their fingers touched, a sizzle of heat ran up her arm and across her shoulders. Paige had to force herself to let go.

"So what did you guys tell Regina's sorority sisters?" Phoebe asked. "They must have been wigging out."

"None of them saw that . . . thing . . . whatever it was, so the official story is a jealousy-crazed ex-boyfriend," Micah said. "I'm pretty sure they bought it."

"Good cover," Piper said, pushing her hands into the back pockets of her jeans and looking at Phoebe. "We should remember that."

"Well, anyway, I just wanted to come by and thank you again for what you did last night," Micah said. He blushed slightly and scoffed at himself, looking at Paige. "I guess I've never been around superheroes before."

Paige laughed, her face turning crimson. "We are *so* not superheroes."

"Well, you were from where I was standing," Micah said. He glanced down at his gold watch and grimaced. "I'd better get going, actually. I have someplace I need to be. But thanks again."

"Anytime," Piper said. "Though we hope you won't ever need us again," she added with a laugh.

Micah took a step toward the door, then looked over at Paige. Yet again, she was shocked by the affect his gaze had on her. She actually had to lean against the wall for support.

"Actually, Paige . . . do you mind if I . . . talk to you for a sec?" he asked.

"Uh . . . sure," Paige said, raising one shoulder. When her sisters didn't immediately flee the room, she walked over to the door and opened it for him. "Let's talk outside."

Micah lifted his hand in parting and slid past Paige onto the front step. She walked out behind him, closed the door, and leaned back against it.

"So . . . ," Paige said awkwardly, clueless as to what Micah might need to say to her in private, though she did have some seriously improbable fantasies flitting through her brain at that moment.

"Paige . . . I know this is going to seem a little forward, considering I just learned your name," Micah said, standing so close to her, she could feel the warmth coming off his body. "But I was wondering if . . . well . . . if you'd like to go out with me tonight."

Paige could have done a few cartwheels right there, but she restrained herself. "Aren't you . . . uh . . . *with* Regina?" she asked, putting her hands behind the small of her back so he wouldn't see how they were fluttering.

Micah smiled slightly and looked up at the sky as if he was searching for the right words.

"Regina is nice," he said finally. "But I haven't felt for her in three dates what I felt for you the moment I saw you last night."

All the air rushed out of Paige's body. Was he kidding? Did people really say stuff like that? And if they did, where had they been all her life?

"Okay, I'll go out with you," Paige said, looking up at him through her thick lashes. "On one condition."

"What's that?" Micah asked.

"You lose the cheesy lines," Paige shot back.

Micah laughed, and Paige was pleased to see a little embarrassed blush color his cheeks. Hey, she couldn't let him think she was swept off her feet before the first date even happened.

"It's a deal," Micah said. "I'll pick you up around seven."

"Make it eight," Paige said.

Then she slipped inside the house and closed the door behind her. She waited until he was safely back in his car before she let out an excited squeal. So she hadn't imagined the attraction in his eyes the night before. And now she was going to go out with the guy who had played a starring role in all of her dreams last night.

"Phoebe was right," Paige said to herself with a grin. "Love does come along when you least expect it."

Chapter

4

"Well . . . that was cool of him—stopping by to thank us," Phoebe said as she and Piper walked back into the kitchen.

"See?" Piper said. "He's a perfectly nice guy."

The front door slammed and seconds later, Paige came flying into the room and slid in her socks across the floor right into Phoebe's side, wrapping her up in a tight, giddy hug. Phoebe barely had time to catch her breath and hug Paige back before her sister released her again and executed a little twirl in the middle of the kitchen. Piper shot a skeptical look at Phoebe and she knew exactly what Piper was thinking. Paige wasn't exactly the twirling type.

"*Who* is your caffeine supplier and can I have his number?" Phoebe deadpanned.

"He asked me out!" Paige said, practically

floating. "You were right! I stopped looking, and there he was!"

Phoebe's heart twisted in her chest and she shot a concerned glance at Piper. This was not good. It was one thing when Micah was just wandering around out there being his potentially dangerous self, but dating her sister? Phoebe was definitely not comfortable with that.

"And you said yes, I assume, from all the flitting," Piper said, cracking a couple of eggs into a large ceramic bowl.

"Of course I said yes!" Paige said with an incredulous smile. "Did you not *see* him?"

"Yeah, but Paige," Phoebe said, squirming forward in her seat, "are you sure about this? I mean, what do you really know about the guy?"

"Come on!" Paige said with a laugh. "What do you ever really know about a guy when you first go out with him? He's nice, polite, cute, and he definitely knows how to dress."

"All good qualities," Piper said as she went to work on the eggs with her whisk. "But do you know where he lives, what he does for a living, who his friends are?"

"Ah! He's friends with Tyrell!" Paige said triumphantly. "And if he has Tyrell's stamp of approval, he obviously has yours."

Phoebe saw Piper take a deep breath as she realized the truth of this statement. Tyrell and Piper were pretty close. And if Tyrell liked Micah . . .

"Well . . . ," Piper said.

Paige, clearly too elated to care what her sisters were saying anyway, crossed the room and started going through the cereal cabinet, her back to Phoebe and Piper. Phoebe waved her hand to get Piper's attention.

"I have to tell her about the evil vision thing," she mouthed.

"No!" Piper mouthed back in an exaggerated way.

"Why?" Phoebe mouthed.

"Look at her!" Piper said, pointing her eyes in Paige's direction.

Paige was popping Apple Jacks into her mouth, munching and humming all at the same time. Phoebe sighed and resigned herself to silence. Paige was way too happy, and Phoebe didn't want to be the one to bring her down, especially when she didn't have any solid proof that Micah was worthy of a warning.

Paige put the box of Apple Jacks down on the counter and quickly flipped through the newspaper. When she got to the bottom of the pile she stopped, confused, and flipped through it again. "Uh, guys? Where's the entertainment section?" she asked.

Phoebe's face fell. She leaned over and tipped open the top of the metal garbage can. There, sitting on top of a pile of apple peels, coffee grounds, and soaked paper towels, was the crumpled-up, brown, wet entertainment section.

"Sorry," Phoebe said. "Little accident."

"Great," Paige said, rolling her eyes, then focusing down on the counter. "And I notice the style section and the food section survived the massacre."

"Sorry, Paige, really," Phoebe said. "It wasn't intentional."

Paige picked up the cereal box again. "Whatever," she said, shaking her head back as she shook off her disappointment as well. "I have better things to think about, anyway. Like what I'm gonna wear tonight." She dug into the box for another handful of cereal and tramped out of the kitchen, clearly a lot less boisterous than she'd been moments before.

"I told you," Piper said, dumping her egg mixture into the skillet. "Grumpy."

Phoebe sighed and looked down at the newspaper in front of her. She was about to shove the local section aside and go straight for style when a picture right on the fold caught her eye. She picked up the page and unfolded it, laying it out flat on the counter. "I don't believe it," she said, staring down at the photo.

"What?" Piper asked.

Phoebe held it up for Piper to see. There, in the middle of the front page, was a full-color picture of a smiling Micah shaking hands with the California governor.

"No way," Piper said.

Phoebe turned the paper around again and read the caption beneath the photo aloud.

"'Millionaire and well-known philanthropist Micah Grant, shown at last week's Friends of the State Awards with Governor Stiles, will cut the red ribbon at the opening of the new children's wing at Mercy Hospital at noon today. Grant raised more than half the donated funds for the state-of-the-art facility.'"

"Wow," Piper said, impressed. "I guess that's why you thought you'd seen him before. He's probably in the news all the time."

Phoebe barely heard Piper, however. She was too busy devouring the short article that accompanied the photo. "It says he's donated to many diverse causes, including area halfway houses and shelters," Phoebe said, growing more and more chagrined with each word she read. "He moved into the area a few years back and started up the Micah Grant Foundation, which works to improve programming for underprivileged kids."

"Call the police. He must be stopped," Piper said sarcastically.

"I guess you were right," Phoebe said, a bit disconcerted. She folded the newspaper up and sighed. "It looks like Paige found a good one."

"Don't sound so excited," Piper said as she folded her omelette in the pan and took it off the stove.

"I am. I'm happy for her," Phoebe responded, trying to sound convincing. Unfortunately, even though all the facts were for him, Phoebe couldn't shake the feeling that there was something off about Micah Grant. She just hoped she was wrong . . . for Paige's sake.

Paige had to concentrate to keep her jaw from falling open in awe when she and Micah walked into the restaurant that evening. Set back in a secluded hill at the top of a deserted one-lane road, the place afforded a breathtaking view of the hills and the bay beyond, magnified by the fact that three of the dining room's four walls were made of floor-to-ceiling glass. The decor was elegant and understated. Each table was draped with a white linen tablecloth and centered by three white candles of various sizes. Rose petals were strewn on the tabletops, and the atmosphere was hushed—romantic. Even the waiters were speaking in whispered tones as they floated from one table to the next in their sleek tuxedos.

"This is unbelievable," Paige whispered as Micah removed her silk wrap, exposing her bare shoulders.

"So are you," Micah said into her ear, sending a chill down her neck.

"What did we say about cheesy lines?" Paige asked, arching her eyebrows and somehow managing to sound totally calm and collected. It was an accomplishment considering how blown away she already was by Micah's sense of style, sense of romance, sense of everything. He'd picked her up in a black limousine, offering a single perfect lily. When he'd given her his arm to walk her to the car, even Phoebe had been impressed.

"Sorry," Micah said with a smile. "I forgot. It's an occupational hazard."

Before Paige could ask him what, exactly, he meant by that, a slim, distinguished-looking man walked over to them and slipped Paige's wrap from Micah's arm. "Your table is ready, Mr. Grant," he said with a slight bow.

Paige and Micah followed him to a secluded corner table right next to the window wall that looked out over the water. Paige was shaking a bit from vertigo as she sat down, but it passed quickly and she looked out at the world, dumbfounded by the beauty of it all.

"I take it you like the restaurant," Micah said, handing her a menu.

"It's okay," Paige joked, raising one shoulder and prompting a laugh from Micah. Paige grinned back. She was so happy that he had a good sense of humor. There was just no point in dating someone who didn't. Even if he did look like he'd just stepped off a Paris runway.

"So, why are cheesy lines an occupational hazard?" Paige asked, glancing up from her menu. "Do you date women for a living?"

"Not quite," Micah said. "I inherited a lot of money from my parents, so I don't really *need* to make a living. Instead, I run a charitable foundation for underprivileged kids, and that involves a lot of schmoozing, to say the least. You have to learn exactly what you need to say to certain people to get them to donate."

"The cause isn't enough to get people to open their wallets?" Paige asked.

"Unfortunately not, in most cases," Micah said with a tight smile. "I wish it were. But I do what I can. We run a few orphanages and a halfway house. I try to go around as much as possible and meet the kids. It reminds me of why I'm popping caviar with obnoxious old ladies every night."

He took a sip of his water and looked down at the menu. Paige could tell he was uncomfortable talking about the money-grubbing part of his job, which just made her like him more. A lot of people would enjoy air-kissing with San Francisco's elite more than fraternizing with penniless kids.

"What do you do?" Micah asked a few moments later. "It doesn't involve obnoxious old ladies, does it?"

"Sometimes," Paige said with a laugh. "I'm a social worker. I work a lot with families of abuse . . . people on welfare . . . I meet some not-so-nice people. But more often I meet the greatest people in the world."

"Exactly," Micah said, his face brightening. "See? You get it. I know exactly what you mean."

They shared a smile and eventually, Paige had to look down at her menu to keep from completely overheating. It was too bad the maître d' couldn't open up one of these window walls and help her cool off a bit. At this point, her strapless dress felt more like a wool sweater.

Micah tore his eyes away as well, opened his menu, and quickly looked it over. "So . . . what kind of food does Paige Matthews like?" he asked, taking another sip from his water glass.

"Well, *not* fish," she answered. "No crab, no clams, no lobsters. Nothing that ever swam, sat on, or crawled along the bottom of the sea."

"Duly noted," Micah said with a smirk, clearly amused by her blunt honesty.

"But I *love* risotto," Paige said, happy to see that there were a few different kinds listed on the menu. "And lamb." She raised her hand apologetically. "I know! They're too cute to eat, but I try not to think about it."

"That's a good policy," Micah said, closing his menu. "You have to have some guilty pleasures. Like me and science-fiction novels. I can't help myself."

Paige sucked in a breath and looked at him skeptically. "Oh, no. I'm out with a sci-fi geek? This could be a deal-breaker," she deadpanned. "Which kind—*Lost in Space* or *The X-Files*?"

"*Star Wars,* actually," Micah answered. "The old ones, not the new."

"Oh well, that's okay, then," Paige said, feigning relief. They both laughed, and Paige found herself unable to stop smiling. *This is going well. Really, really well.*

"So, what do you like to read?" Micah asked, leaning his elbows on the table. "I bet you're into romance novels."

"Oh, please," Paige scoffed, rolling her eyes. "My sister Phoebe reads them like they're going out of style. Which they already did—decades ago. I'm more into the classics. I love Austen and I've been reading a lot of Willa Cather lately."

"So you *are* into romance novels," Micah said, smiling slightly. "Just really old ones."

"Hey! Those are relevant books," Paige said. But she couldn't make herself protest more. After all, the guy was right. But how was she supposed to know that a man like Micah would have a clue what Austen and Cather wrote about? It was usually a safe bet that a guy would let that revelation slide by with a fake nod of understanding, not wanting to say something wrong and reveal that he didn't know the first thing about literature.

Suddenly, the waiter appeared at their table so silently, he could have been beamed there. "Are you ready to order?" he asked, leaning slightly toward the table.

"Yes. We'll both have the lamb," Micah said, handing him their menus. "And . . . Paige, did you choose a risotto?"

"I'll have the pumpkin," Paige told the waiter with a smile.

"That sounds good," Micah said, his blue eyes sparkling. "Bring two, please."

Paige folded her arms on the table in front of her and looked Micah in the eye, which wasn't easy. Every time she did it she felt as if she were going to asphyxiate from the butterfly frenzy in her chest. "What's the deal, Grant? Can't make up your mind for yourself?" she asked.

"Maybe I just want to know everything about you," Micah said without a pause. "And that means knowing exactly how the food you love tastes."

Paige was flattered right down to her toenails, but she tried not to show it. "By that logic are you going to go home, read *Sense and Sensibility*, slip into a pair of pink flannel pajamas, and listen to a little Kiss?"

Micah smiled a slow, sexy smile and leaned in so close to Paige, she could smell the minty scent of his breath. "If that's what it takes," he said, "then that's what I'll do."

Suddenly Paige was engulfed in a wave of dizziness so strong, her eyes clouded over with prickly gray dots. She felt her skin flush with heat and leaned back in her chair, discreetly taking in a long, deep breath. For the past twenty-four hours she'd been marveling at the effects Micah had on her, but this was a whole new level of intense.

"Are you all right?" Micah asked, his dark brows creased with concern.

"I'm fine," Paige said, taking a sip of water and lifting her hair off the back of her neck. "I think it's just the height . . . the view . . . you know? It's a little . . . overwhelming."

It sounded like a good excuse. It was, in fact, a *perfect* excuse. And Micah called the maître d' over and asked if they could be moved away from the window. The man was all too solicitous, and within moments he was leading Paige to a new table in the back of the room.

Paige, while relieved that the excuse had been convincing, couldn't have been more freaked out as she followed the man to her new table, acutely aware of Micah walking behind her. She was freaked because she knew it hadn't been vertigo or dizziness that had taken over her. It had been Micah. There was no other explanation for the force of what she had felt.

Paige was falling in love.

Later that night, Micah quietly opened the door of a hulking old mansion in one of the oldest neighborhoods in town. Paige tiptoed as quietly as possible as she stepped over the threshold into the orphanage and she was surprised the moment she took a look around. Somehow she'd been imagining a place like the orphanage in *Annie*, but this house was more like the one Daddy Warbucks owned than the run-down hole Miss Hannigan ran.

"*This* is an orphanage?" Paige whispered, taking in the gleaming floors and the colorful art decorating the walls.

"When we're here we just call it a home," Micah whispered back. "It makes the kids feel less different."

They walked through the entryway together, heading for an elevator that blended in with the cream-colored walls.

"Do you bring all your dates here?" Paige asked, walking backward so she could smile up at him.

"Well, you wanted to learn more about my work, and this is my favorite part," Micah replied, hitting the UP button on the wall.

The elevator doors slid open, and Paige stepped inside. Moments later, she and Micah walked out onto the fifth floor—a long hallway lined with thick carpeting. As they strolled along in silence, Paige noticed that each room was decorated with handmade signs with children's names on them.

"Did the kids make these?" she asked, gently touching her fingertips to a drawing of a blue whale with the name "Jonah" written above it in gold glitter.

"Yeah, Jonah was pretty psyched about the whole Jonah and the Whale story," Micah replied with a small smile. "We let them decorate their rooms themselves, too—as much as we can. It's not like we have an endless budget for each kid, but at least they get to personalize things a bit. Makes it feel more like a home."

He walked her to the end of the hall and then pressed his finger to his lips before quietly opening the door to the last room. Paige peeked inside and saw four little boys fast asleep on four tiny beds. The shaft of light from the hallway illuminated a cherubic face sticking out from the sheets of the closest bed. Paige watched as Micah's face softened at the sight of the boy.

"That's Christopher," he whispered. "He's been having trouble sleeping lately, so I just wanted to check on him."

Paige felt as if her heart were growing inside her chest. She couldn't believe how much Micah clearly cared about each of these kids. He knew their stories, their sleeping habits. He'd brought a date here so he could check on one of them. *Where did this guy come from?* she wondered.

"Okay, where's the catch?" Paige asked once Micah had quietly clicked the door closed.

"Catch?" Micah asked, his brow knitting.

He started down the hall again and pulled out a tiny key when they'd reached the closed glass doors to the veranda at the end of the hall. He unlocked one of the doors and stood aside so that Paige could step out before him. Paige took in a long breath of the fresh night air and leaned her arms onto the railing, looking out at the peaceful street below.

"The catch," she repeated, smiling lightly as a breeze lifted her hair from her shoulders. "You seem just a little bit too perfect. There has to be something wrong with you."

Micah laughed and joined her, leaning his arms onto the railing. "There's something wrong with everyone," he said. "You just have to decide whether you can see past a person's flaws."

"Well, I haven't found any in you yet," Paige said, looking into his magnetic eyes.

"Then it should be easy for you to look past them," Micah said, sliding closer to her.

His arm brushed hers, and that incredible warmth she'd felt earlier in the evening overtook her again. She closed her eyes as the gray cloud shaded her vision. When she opened them again, Micah's face was millimeters from hers. Paige's heart seized up in her chest, and all the air rushed out of her.

"I'm going to kiss you now," he said quietly. "If that's okay."

Paige couldn't have answered if she'd tried, so instead she closed the distance between them and touched her lips to his. The moment she did, her knees went out from under her, but Micah wrapped his arms around her and kept her from falling. For the first time in her life, Paige knew what people meant by an out-of-body experience. Micah's kiss made her float—it made her leave herself.

And as far as she was concerned, she didn't care if she never came back down.

Chapter 5

Piper sat at one of the corner booths at P3 on Monday afternoon with her checkbook, accounting logs, and about a thousand receipts and bills spread out on the surface of the smooth table in front of her. She hated the financial part of her job with a passion, but just couldn't seem to get up the guts to let it go to some faceless accountant. Still, whenever she sat down to do the books, she found herself considering it all over again. Especially when the splitting headache started to set in.

"Ugh! There has to be a better way!" Piper exclaimed to the empty club, pulling her glasses off and tossing them down on the table. She pinched the bridge of her nose and closed her eyes. "Why did I have to be born such a control freak?"

"Need some aspirin, boss?"

Piper jumped at the unexpected sound of Tyrell's voice. "Yeah, and a defibrillator, thank you very much!!" she said, holding her hand over her heart and glaring up at him. "You scared me into cardiac arrest."

A boyish smile lit Tyrell's dark features, and he brought his hands out from behind his back. He placed a glass of water and two tiny pills on the table next to her glasses. Piper felt relieved just looking at the painkillers.

"You're forgiven," she said, reaching for the glass. "So . . . where did you come from?" she asked as she popped the aspirin in her mouth.

"I came in the back a few minutes ago," Tyrell said, pointing over his shoulder. "I've been banging around in the kitchen for a while now. You didn't hear me?"

Piper sighed, pushing her hands into her hair as she stared down at the mess of paper in front of her. "I guess I was just too engrossed by what I was doing."

"Well, I don't want to get you off track," Tyrell said, taking a step back. "I was just going to inventory the cleaning supplies and see if we need anything."

"Tyrell, hold on a sec," Piper said before he could slip away. She felt a little twinge of guilt over what she was about to do, but she ignored it. After all, Paige was her sister. It was perfectly normal—even admirable—to look out for her. Tyrell hovered at the opposite end of the table, waiting for her to speak. "Tell me about your friend Micah Grant," Piper said finally.

Tyrell's whole face lit up. "That's right! I was going to ask you if he ever came by yesterday. He's a great guy."

"Oh, yeah?" Piper said, raising one eyebrow. "How so?"

"Well . . . you know I didn't have an easy time of it as a kid—even just a few years back," Tyrell said. "Micah ran the halfway house where I ended up finally getting clean. He was always there visiting, hanging with us, taking us out to games and stuff. And he didn't have to do that, you know? He's got tons of money, but he was always hanging out with us. I think that really helped me turn it around—seeing how much people could care."

"Huh," Piper said with a smile. With a glowing report like that, she might as well go home tonight and give Paige her wedding dress. "Thanks, Tyrell. He does sound like a great guy."

"Out of curiosity, why did he want to find you guys, anyway?" Tyrell asked, crossing his arms over his chest.

"Oh . . . well . . ."

He wanted to thank us for vanquishing a demon and saving his life?

"He wanted to ask Paige out, actually," she said quickly, glad that there was such a perfect excuse readily available.

"Paige and Micah?" Tyrell exclaimed with a grin. "That's great!"

At that moment, Paige came bounding down the stairs into the club and jumped the last few steps, landing on the floor with a thump. "Oh, it's great all right!" she exclaimed.

Piper couldn't help smiling at the sight of her rosy-cheeked sister. The girl looked like a fourteen-year-old who'd just kissed her first middle-school crush. She was even wearing a little plaid miniskirt and a bright sweater, which only served to solidify the image.

"What are you doing here in the middle of the day?" Piper asked as Paige quickly crossed the room. Paige plopped onto the soft bench surrounding Piper's table, and Piper bounced up from the force of it.

"What, I can't come see my favorite sister on my lunch break?" Paige asked, wrapping one arm around Piper.

"I'll leave you two alone," Tyrell said, shaking his head as he turned to go. "Paige, I think it's great about you and Micah!" he called out before disappearing into the kitchen.

"Me too!" Paige shouted back.

"So . . . tell me all about it," Piper said, turning toward Paige and resting her elbow on the back of the bench. "I was sorry I missed you this morning."

"I know. I had to get to work early to review a case," Paige said. "But Piper, last night was so unbelievably amazing! He took me to this incredible restaurant and we ate the most scrumptious food and then we went and visited one of the orphanages he runs and then we went dancing. . . ."

"Wow. What time did you get home?" Piper asked.

"About an hour before I had to get up for work," Paige admitted with a laugh. "But it was so worth it. He's incredible. He's so caring and funny and polite and, well, I'm not proud to admit it, but he pretty much turns me to mush."

"That sounds like one heck of a first date," Piper said, resting her cheek in her hand. "My first dates usually ended with me hovering over a box of tissues wondering where it all went wrong."

Paige laughed. "Well . . . now you have Leo," she said, looking wistfully across the room toward the dance floor. "And I have Micah."

A little red flag suddenly popped up in Piper's mind. There was something about the far-off look in Paige's eyes that was just . . . unnatural—almost blank. And the fact that Paige was already comparing her and Micah with Piper and Leo—two people who'd known each other for years and had been married for months—was a bit much.

"Uh . . . you're not thinking of running off to Vegas or anything, are you?" Piper asked, only half-kidding.

"No!" Paige exclaimed, whacking Piper's knee as she snapped out of her little trance. "But he *is* taking me out again tonight. He wants to show me his place."

Red flag number two. "His place?" Piper asked, sitting up straight. "You guys just met two days ago. Isn't it a little early for him to be showing you his . . . *place*?"

"Please, Piper! This is the twenty-first century!" Paige said, laughing again. "And besides, I'm not going to do anything crazy. And Micah's been a perfect gentleman. He just told me he lives in some amazing mansion up in the hills and I said I'd love to see it and so . . . I'm going to see it."

"I don't know, Paige. I mean . . . are you sure you want to put yourself in that position?" Piper asked, squirming a bit at the parental tone of her own voice. "I mean, alone with a guy in his big old mansion, which, by the way, how does he afford? Do you have any idea where his money comes from or—"

"I don't believe this!" Paige exclaimed suddenly, her face the picture of indignation. "I meet a completely perfect guy and all you and Phoebe can do is try to find the flaws!"

"Paige, I—"

"What's next? Are you going to accuse him of being evil like Phoebe did?" Paige asked, pushing herself out of the booth.

"No! In fact, from what Tyrell told me, Micah *is* an amazing person!" Piper said. "I just want you to be careful, that's all."

"Great! So now you're asking questions about Micah behind my back," Paige said, grabbing her bag off the bench. "I know Phoebe is all wigged out about her vision, but I thought at least *you* would be happy for me."

Paige turned and stalked across the room, and Piper slid along the bench and out of the booth. "Paige! Paige, come on! I was only looking out for you!"

"Yeah, well, don't bother!" Paige said as she tramped up the stairs. She never paused or looked back.

Piper sighed in frustration and raised one hand to her head, which was now pounding even more painfully. She could actually feel a vein throbbing in her forehead. Slowly, she lowered herself down onto the bench again and took a deep breath.

"What is wrong with me?" she asked herself under her breath. "Tyrell loves the guy. Paige loves the guy. So why do I suddenly feel like we can't trust him?"

It made no sense. Yesterday she'd been perfectly willing to wish Paige and Micah happy dating, and now . . . now she was acting like Phoebe. Going with a gut instinct that had no basis in reality. But there was something about the way Paige had talked about him . . . something about the dazed expression on her face when she'd momentarily spaced out . . . something about it all made the little hairs on the back of Piper's neck stand on end.

"Get a grip. This is not reality," Piper told herself, shaking her head. She lifted her glasses and slipped them back onto the bridge of her nose. Then she picked up one of the bills from the table and started to review it. *This* is reality . . . unfortunately."

Phoebe cranked up the volume on the portable stereo in the corner of the basement and tilted her head back and forth a few times, cracking her neck as she bounced up and down on the balls of her feet. Paige had left a little while ago for her second date with Micah, Piper was working at the club, and Cole was still MIA. What with her distrust of Paige's new man and the fact that Cole was out there somewhere, possibly in mortal peril, Phoebe had more than enough negative energy to expend. All she could think about was kicking a little butt.

Phoebe was already sweating from the workout she'd given herself and her arm muscles were starting to quiver like jelly, but she hadn't quite worked out all the confused aggression she had pumping through her veins. The punching bag was in for another good beating.

Micah . . . Cole . . . Paige . . . random demons chasing Cole . . .

Suddenly, the Aplacum and its evil claws flashed through Phoebe's mind, and she released a low growl of anger as she let a punch fly, landing it in the center of the heavy bag. Once she got started, she just kept punching faster and faster and faster, throwing in a roundhouse kick or two for good measure. She kept seeing the Aplacum lunging at her, advancing on Regina. Kept hearing its deafening growl.

It's gone. It can't hurt anyone. It's gone, it's gone, it's gone. . . .

Faster and faster and faster Phoebe's arms flew until she was gasping for breath. Until her legs were going to give out beneath her. Until she collapsed forward into the punching bag, hugging it for dear life.

She knew it wasn't the Aplacum that was bothering her. It wasn't even Cole. She knew he could take care of himself. It was that nagging feeling. That feeling that there was some other evil lurking in her vision. That feeling that somehow Micah had something to do with that evil, and the knowledge that her sister was out with the guy right now.

This isn't over, a little voice in Phoebe's mind warned. *The Aplacum was just the beginning.*

"Okay, that's it," Phoebe said, wiping the back of her hand across her brow as she steadied herself.

She flicked the stereo off and climbed the basement stairs to the second floor, and then the stairs to the attic, her legs screaming in protest the whole way. By the time she got to *The Book of Shadows,* she had to pull it down off its podium and sit down on the window seat.

Cracking the book open on the bench next to her, Phoebe leaned her shoulder against the cool glass surface of the window and started to flip through the pages. She had to make sure she hadn't missed anything. When she finally found the Aplacum, she quickly looked over the page again. No new information had magically appeared. It was still just a scary-looking demon with no motive and a vanquishing spell. Easy as one-two-poof.

Frustrated, Phoebe turned the page to the next demon and almost winced. This drawing was no prettier than the last. It pictured a great hulking creature with a face that looked as if it had been mummified for a thousand years. Deep, fleshy wrinkles, hundreds of sharp vampirelike teeth, and blank black eyes stared back at her. Its hands were stretched out at its sides, and beams of some kind were emanating from its wrists.

"'Vandalus,'" Phoebe read, running her finger across the word at the top of the page. "Hope we never encounter you."

She was about to flip the page once again when something caught her eye. The word "Aplacum" right in the center of the description of Vandalus. Phoebe's heart instantly started to pound. She pulled the book onto her lap and began to read. This could be it. This could be the answer she was looking for.

"Vandalus, one of the most violent, destructive demons of the underworld, fought for centuries against its arch nemesis Aplacum for domination of the dimensions. If one ever killed the other, the vanquishing demon would reign supreme, bringing untold horrors to all humanity."

Phoebe paused and took a deep breath. "They sound like a lovely couple," she said.

"Fortunately, the Elders managed to lure Vandulus away from his loyal minions long enough to cast a powerful spell on him, banishing him to Earth in the early nineteenth century."

"Banishing him to Earth?" Phoebe said, her brow knitting. "Wouldn't we notice if we had *that* thing walking around somewhere?"

Confused and intrigued, Phoebe read on, learning more about the war between Aplacum and Vandalus. She was so engrossed that when she turned the page again, what she saw shocked her like a bucket of cold water being dumped over her head.

"Oh, no," Phoebe said, her heart pounding. "No. This can't be."

Chapter

6

Paige sat back in the cushy limousine seat, concentrating hard to keep her face from betraying her excitement. She smoothed down the silky skirt of her red gown and took a deep, soothing breath, looking out the window with an expression of complete serenity.

It lasted for about three seconds.

Before she even realized it, Paige was on the edge of her seat again, giving her heart free reign to pound around as much as it wanted. When she'd left the house that night, she'd been concerned that she might not be able to get Phoebe and Piper's words of caution out of her mind, but she hadn't thought about her sisters in hours. She was too busy being excited.

The car stopped at a red light, and Paige's toe began to tap against the carpeted floor. Micah chuckled, and she glanced over at him out of the corner of her eye. He was sitting casually in the corner, his arm draped along the top of the seat, his temple resting on the fingertips of his other hand. He smiled when he saw Paige glance his way.

"How can you be so calm?!" Paige asked, throwing her hands up. "We're going to a premiere! A real movie premiere . . . in L.A. . . . with *stars*."

Paige had been waiting to turn into a pumpkin ever since Micah had ushered her onto his private jet earlier that evening. As soon as he'd sat her down in a leather airplane seat that was bigger and more comfortable than the couch in her childhood living room, he'd told her he'd been given two tickets to the opening of a new action flick in Hollywood . . . and then he'd *apologized*. Apparently he'd thought that action movies wouldn't be Paige's thing.

She'd corrected him as politely as possible. It didn't matter what the movie was. She was going to be rubbing elbows with real, live celebrities.

"They're just people," Micah said with a quick shrug.

"Oh, please," Paige scoffed, slumping back and crossing her arms over her chest. "You're only able to be so casual about this because you've done it a million times."

"I suppose," Micah said, unconvinced.

"Come on. You can't tell me that you didn't get a *little* psyched the first time you were invited to one of these things," Paige prompted.

Micah cracked a slow grin and leaned in toward her a bit, a lock of his dark brown hair falling over his eye. "Okay. Maybe a little."

His closeness sent a little shiver of delight down Paige's spine, and she had to bite her lip to keep from grinning too broadly. How had she gotten so lucky? Not only did she meet the most incredible guy ever, but now he was whisking her away to Hollywood! And all because of a little vision Phoebe had. Paige made a mental note to thank her sister as soon as possible.

The limousine rolled to a stop, and Paige's heart hit her stomach. She looked out the window and found herself gazing down a long red carpet that was flanked on either side by about a thousand screaming fans. Flashing lightbulbs blinded her, and her pulse was racing so quickly, she was sure she was about to faint.

"You ready?" Micah asked.

"Unnnh," came the reply.

Micah opened his door and slammed it, knocking Paige out of her stupor. She straightened the straps on her dress and pressed her lips together, then pushed her hair behind her shoulders just before Micah opened her door. Paige stepped one foot out onto the asphalt, shaking like she'd just gotten out of the ocean on a cold night. Micah offered her his hand and she gladly took it. If she didn't, she would have definitely been kissing red carpet.

"How do you feel?" Micah asked, slipping his arm through hers as she looked around uncertainly.

"Like a poser," she answered under her breath. "No one here cares about us."

"These people are going to take one look at you, figure you're the new starlet in the movie, and beg for your attention," Micah said, his deep voice close enough to her ear to send yet another thrill down her spine.

She laughed at his delusional claim, but it was enough of an ego boost to get her walking. Paige clung to Micah's arm as they slowly made their way down the red carpet. At first she had to make herself smile, the effort almost painful. But the closer she got to the open theater doors, the more natural it became. Apparently people *did* care that they were there. Some of the paparazzi called out Micah's name, and he paused so they could snap a few pictures of him and Paige. By the time they'd ducked into the opulent theater, Paige was positively glowing. She couldn't see anything past the flashbulb shadows floating in front of her eyes, but for the first time in her life she knew how it felt to be a movie star.

"See? That wasn't so bad, was it?" Micah asked, planting a quick kiss on her forehead.

Paige smiled up at him, her heart fluttering. "It definitely didn't suck."

Later that evening, as Micah drove his convertible through the winding streets of San Francisco, Paige was floating on a cloud of happiness. She'd just spent an entire evening chatting with celebrities, eating the most intensely amazing food (aside from Piper's), and being waited on hand-and-foot by the best-looking guy in the room, male models and A-list actors included.

"I had an incredible time tonight," Paige breathed, tipping her head back to look up at the full moon that hung low in the night sky.

"It's not over yet," Micah said. He reached out his hand to cover hers, and the warmth from his skin seemed to travel over her entire body.

"That's right," she said with a smile. "I'm going to get to see your place."

"Yes, you are," Micah said, returning his hand to the wheel as he made a particularly sharp turn. "I just hope you like it."

I'm sure I will, Paige thought. Anyone as completely perfect as Micah had to have one amazing abode. Unless, of course, he turned out to be one of those closet frat boys with empty pizza boxes, beer-can castles, and stacks of dirty magazines all over the place. But somehow, looking at his classic profile and his perfectly gelled hair, she doubted it.

As the car wove its way farther and farther from the center of town and higher and higher into the hills, Paige leaned back and let herself enjoy the moment. It was a perfect warm night, the wind was in her hair, and by the looks of the estates the car was zipping by, Micah lived in one seriously posh neighborhood. She felt more like a movie star now than she had at any other point in the evening.

Micah pulled the car to a stop at the rounded edge of a dead end and put it into park. There wasn't a single sound except for the idling car engine. Paige looked up at the huge iron gate in front of her and felt her jaw drop just the slightest bit.

"A little paranoid?" she joked.

"I know, it's kind of gothic," Micah said with a laugh. "But the gate's been here as long as the house has. It's part of its history. I couldn't tear it down."

He reached into his breast pocket, pulled out a slim key card, and inserted it into a silver box built into the brick wall that ran from either side of the gate. There was a quiet beep and then the iron gates opened with a deafening clang.

"Where, exactly, *is* the house?" Paige asked, squinting into the darkness as Micah pulled his car through the slowly parting gates.

"You'll see it in just a minute," he answered.

Sure enough, when Micah pulled the car around a wide turn, the "house" loomed into view at the very top of the hill. It was more like a mansion than a house, and Paige felt a chill as she took it all in. Built in the classic Victorian style so popular in the San Francisco area, the structure was sprawling. With an immense wraparound deck, at least four gables, and a garage big enough to fit the Halliwell Manor inside, Micah's home could actually have been classified as an estate.

It was also dark, dreary, and intimidating enough to play the starring role in an old ghost movie.

"It's incredible," Paige said, gazing up at the very tip-top of the highest turret. "It's like something out of a Brontë novel."

"I'm glad you like it," Micah said, pulling his car up to the front door, the tires crunching along the gravel drive. "It's been in the family forever."

"You must have some family," Paige said.

She popped open the car door and climbed out, never taking her eyes off the house. Her mind was already conjuring up a tragically romantic scenario to go along with the storybook mansion. A woman in eighteenth-century garb, staring mournfully out at the stars from her room on the fourth floor, wishing for a way to escape the marriage her father had planned for her so that she could be with her true love. Her lover, attempting to climb the gables to rescue her, only to fall to his death just before their fingers met at her window.

It was all too easy to see.

"Come on," Micah said, startling her as he placed his hand on the small of her back. Paige pulled her flimsy red shawl tighter around her shoulders. "Let's go inside."

Lifting her skirt slightly, Paige climbed the porch steps. The door creaked as Micah opened it and Paige stepped inside, feeling as if she'd stepped into her own vivid imagination. The entrance hall was tiled in an intricate mosaic pattern, depicting the moon eclipsing the sun. A wide, rounded staircase began just above the mosaic, and Paige followed Micah up the steps, gazing around at the haunting artwork and the crystal chandelier that hung above.

Micah led her along the upstairs hallway, opening doors as they went along. Each bedroom was decorated in the Victorian style, as if they hadn't been touched since the original owners had made their mark. Micah took her to every single room, reverently explaining the layout of the house and the antiques each chamber possessed. An hour had passed before they descended once again to the first floor and Micah ushered Paige into his library.

"I'm sure you already know this, but I have to tell you, your home is beautiful," Paige said, walking along the periphery of the library, taking in the leather-bound titles as Micah followed closely behind.

"And I'm sure you already know this, but so are you," Micah said.

Paige's heart skipped a beat and she turned to look at him, blushing furiously. His eyes were completely sincere, and she found herself uncharacteristically averting her gaze. Micah reached up and touched her cheek with his finger-tips, causing her heart to skip even faster.

"It was so important to me that you love this place as much as I do," he continued quietly. "But I knew. I knew the moment you saw it that you had fallen in love."

A warm rush raced over Paige's skin as he moved his hands to her waist. She looked up at him, her eyelids heavy. "How could I not?" she said. "It's . . . fascinating."

As they gazed into each other's eyes, Paige felt the same dizzying sensation she'd experi-enced at the restaurant the night before, but it was okay. She was beginning to enjoy it—this feeling of being lost in his eyes.

"You haven't even seen the best part yet," Micah said, his voice throaty.

"The best part?" she repeated, temporarily incapable of forming her own thoughts.

"The garden," Micah said, his eyes flashing with excitement. "You have to see the garden."

He moved away from her, and Paige sud-denly felt cold and alert, as if she'd just been slapped in the face. The dizziness was gone, and her senses seemed to have returned in full force. She shook her head a bit to lessen the shock to her system. Micah was striding toward the back of the room and a pair of glass doors that led out onto a stone-floored patio. Suddenly, as caught up as she was in the gothic romance of it all, Paige felt incredibly exhausted.

"It's actually getting a little late," Paige said, glancing down at her watch. "And I assume the gardens at a place like this are kind of huge. Can we do it another time?"

Micah paused, his back to her, and Paige bit her lip uncertainly. It seemed to her to be an easy question to answer. Why was he taking so much time to process it? "Micah?" she prompted.

He finally turned, a smile lighting his handsome features. "I saved the best for last," he said, holding out his hand. "We don't have to take a tour of the whole grounds. I just want you to see it. It's my favorite part of the estate."

Paige looked at his outstretched hand and sighed. "Well, if it's your *favorite* part," she said with a grin, pushing her fatigue aside.

She took his hand and he closed his fingers tightly around hers, then reached for the brass knob on the garden door.

And then, Paige's cell phone rang.

"Damn. Sorry," Paige said, pulling her hand away. She popped open her evening bag and pulled out her tiny phone. The Caller ID read HOME.

"It's just my sister," she said to Micah, who shoved his hands in his pockets. "It'll only be a sec."

Paige hit the TALK button and brought the phone to her ear. "I'm kinda on a date here," she said through her teeth, turning away from Micah.

"Paige, it's an emergency," Piper's voice sliced through the earpiece. "You need to come home. Now."

Paige felt her heart freeze up with fear. It was rare for Piper to sound so freaked. What had happened? Had Cole been caught by the Source's bounty hunters? Had something happened to Phoebe? Paige was dying to ask, but she knew better than to try to have a Charmed Ones conversation in front of a civilian spectator like Micah. Even if he *had* seen one demon, a lot of what Paige and her sisters dealt with was more than regular people could handle.

"I'll be right there," Paige said. She turned and looked at Micah apologetically. "I'm so sorry," she said, shoving her phone back in her bag. "There's an emergency at home. I have to go."

"Are you sure?" Micah asked.

"Believe me, I wouldn't leave unless I had to," Paige said, honestly. She took a step closer to him and laid her hand on the lapel of his tuxedo jacket. "You don't mind, do you?"

"No," Micah said, with an unconvincingly tight smile. "But if *you* don't mind, I'm going to have Charles take you." He reached past her to a phone on a table against the wall.

"Charles?" she asked, confused.

"My driver," Micah responded, his words clipped. Then he spoke into the phone, looking away from her. "Charles, I need you to take Ms. Matthews home. She has a family emergency."

He hung up and put his hands back in his pockets. "He's bringing the car around."

"Wow. Charles is on call twenty-four/seven? Who are you, Batman?" Paige asked, trying to lighten the mood.

"He's like a member of the family," Micah said flatly. He walked past her over to a desk on the other side of the room and started flipping through some papers. "I'd take you myself, but if we're going to cut the evening short, I'd like to get some work done."

Swallowing hard, Paige walked up next to Micah and tilted her head to try to catch his eye. "I'm really sorry about this," she said tentatively. "I'd like to do it again."

Micah let out an audible breath and finally looked up at her. "I'm sorry," he said, shaking his head. "I'm acting like a baby. I guess that's what happens when I don't get what I want," he added, cracking a sheepish smile.

Paige grinned. She stood on her toes and kissed his lips. It was a long, lingering kiss, and when she stepped away, he kept his eyes closed for an extra moment.

"Next time," she said. "I promise."

A horn honked from out on the drive, and Paige turned to go. As Micah opened the door for her and she stepped out into the night, she felt like Cinderella leaving her prince behind, like she was waking up from a perfect dream.

She sat down in the car and blew Micah a

kiss. He waved in return, a sad little smile playing about his lips. Then Charles put the car in drive and before Paige knew it, she was winding her way down the hill once again.

"Whatever this emergency is," Paige whispered, "it had better be catastrophic."

"Where *is* she?" Piper said through her teeth, pacing back and forth in front of the front window in the attic.

Ever since Phoebe had called Piper home and shown her what she'd found in *The Book of Shadows*, she'd been moving around nonstop. She couldn't handle the idea that Paige was out there somewhere on her own and they had no way of protecting her.

"She'll be here," Phoebe said from her perch on the window seat. She had the book open on her lap in front of her, ready to show Paige what she'd found, and her hands were clutched together on top of the pages. Despite her calming words, it was as if her whole body was coiled with tension.

"Ooh! Headlights!" Piper exclaimed as two beams of white light flashed across the room. She rushed back to the window and saw a limousine pulling to a stop in front of the Manor. The moment Piper saw Paige step out of the limo in one piece, she felt a rush of relief that had the force of a tidal wave. "She's here," she announced.

Phoebe placed the book down next to her and pushed herself up from her seat.

"Hello?" Paige's voice carried up the stairs. "Where are you guys?"

"In the attic!" Phoebe called out.

Paige clomped up the two flights of stairs and entered the room in her floor-length gown, her eyes wide with worry. "What's wrong?" she asked. "Is everyone okay?"

Phoebe, obviously unable to contain herself, grabbed Paige up in a bear hug. Paige shot Piper a questioning look over Phoebe's shoulder.

"Okay. What was *that* about?" Paige asked when Phoebe finally pulled away.

"I'm just so glad you're okay," Phoebe said with a relieved smile, crossing her arms over her waist.

"You're glad that *I'm* okay?" Paige asked, her brow furrowing as she dropped her shawl and tiny purse on the little couch in the center of the room. "I thought there was an emergency *at home.*"

"There is . . . sort of," Piper said, biting her lip.

A shadow flitted across Paige's face as she looked from one sister to the other. "I just left the single most amazing date of my life to run back here. Somebody better start talking."

Piper laced her fingers together and walked up to Paige, clicking her teeth together as she tried to decide exactly how to say what she had

to say. It was a delicate situation, and one she'd
hoped she'd never have to get into—again.
Paige just stood there, hand on hip, clearly
growing more and more impatient for an explanation.

"Maybe you should sit down," Piper suggested.

Paige let out a groan and rolled her eyes
before flopping down on the couch next to her
things. "Okay. Out with it," she said.

"Phoebe was doing some more research on
the Aplacum and she found something . . . not
good," Piper said, glancing at Phoebe.

Paige tucked her chin, looking up at Piper
expectantly. "Which was . . . ?"

Piper lowered herself onto the edge of her
favorite chair, feeling suddenly tired. Looking at
Paige all dressed up, all flushed, all romance-
movie worthy, made telling her this news much
more difficult. The girl had just found the man of
her dreams. Piper couldn't believe that she and
Phoebe were going to have to tear that away.

"Uh . . . Phoebe? Maybe you should explain,"
Piper suggested. After all, Phoebe had some
experience with the subject. She'd been through
this once herself.

"Well, the Aplacum is actually the archenemy
of a demon called Vandalus," Phoebe explained,
crossing to the window to pick up *The Book of
Shadows.* "And Vandalus is seriously nasty. He's
close to being the ultimate evil of the under-

world—capable of mass destruction."

Phoebe paused to let this little fact sink in to Paige's mind, but Paige obviously didn't yet get the weight of the situation. "And?" she prompted, ready to move on.

"*And* he was banished to Earth in human form over a thousand years ago because he was too powerful to destroy," Piper put in.

"There's no drawing in *The Book of Shadows* of what Vandalus looks like in human form," Phoebe said, pausing to take a deep breath and glancing at Piper for moral support. She handed the book to Paige, who lowered it into her lap. "But from the description . . . he sounds a lot like Micah."

There were a few moments of perfect and utter silence, broken only by the sound of the three sisters' breathing. Piper watched, her heart going out to Paige as this news slowly sank in. At first Paige just looked at them blankly, ignoring the book, but then her face registered confusion and shock. She slumped back into the couch in a position that looked totally incongruous with her elegant dress, letting *The Book of Shadows* slip from her lap.

"I don't believe this," she said under her breath.

"I know, honey, it's hard to take in," Phoebe said. She crouched in front of the couch, reached out, and rubbed Paige's arm comfortingly. "But it's going to be okay. We're here for you. I'm sure we can figure out a way to vanquish him."

Paige's mouth dropped open in disbelief. "*Vanquish* him? Are you seriously telling me you want to vanquish my boyfriend?"

Piper's heart dropped like a meteor, and Phoebe looked at her, shocked. "Paige, you can't *go out* with him anymore," Piper said. "He could be seriously dangerous."

"Yeah, right," Paige said with a scoff, sitting up straight. "'The human description of this Vandalus guy sounds a lot like Micah,'" she repeated sarcastically, picking up the book roughly. "What does it say? Tall, dark, and handsome? How many people fit that description?"

Phoebe pulled the book away from Paige and stood. "'As a human, Vandalus is of tall stature, with dark hair and piercing blue eyes. The color is almost unnatural,'" Phoebe read, pacing the room.

"See! That could be anyone!" Paige protested, sitting up straight.

"But that's not even the most incriminating part," Phoebe said. "It says in here that Vandalus would hypnotize children and train them to become part of his army."

Piper looked at Paige, waiting for her to see the connection, but her sister just shook her head and scoffed. "So?"

"So?" Piper repeated, throwing one hand out. "So Micah works with children, making them trust him, making them love him, making them *rely* on him. He's putting together his army."

"Okay, you guys have obviously been playing in the funky side of the magic cabinet," Paige said. "I find a guy who has devoted his life to charity work and you tell me he's raising an army of kids to fulfill his evil plans."

"Yuh-huh!" Piper and Phoebe said in unison.

"Paige, it all makes sense," Piper said, starting to feel desperate. "Think about it. If Aplacum and Vandalus are sworn archenemies, then Aplacum was probably there to kill Micah, not Regina."

Paige blinked and, for a moment, Piper thought she had her on the logic front, but her sister's silence didn't last long.

"Well, then why did Phoebe see the Aplacum killing *Regina* in her vision?" Paige shot back, crossing her arms over her chest and shooting them a triumphant look. "And the Charmed Ones don't normally get visions sending them off to stop demon-on-demon killings, do they?"

"Uh, no," Phoebe said, her brow creasing as she hugged *The Book of Shadows* against her chest.

"Well . . . clearly Regina was going to be a casualty before Aplacum got to Micah," Piper said, raising her chin, proud and a bit surprised at having come up with a good answer on the spot. "Phoebe must have gotten the vision so that we'd save the innocent and she wouldn't get caught in the crossfire."

"Okay, I've had just about enough of this," Paige said, slapping her hands onto the couch cushions at her sides and pushing herself up. "I mean, I can take the little slights from you guys here and there, but this is getting outta hand."

"What do you mean, 'little slights'?" Piper demaded.

"I *mean*, you guys obviously don't want me to be happy!" Paige announced incredulously. She grabbed her tiny bag and rummaged through it, trembling with anger. It suddenly slipped from her hand and hit the floor, sending makeup, cell phone, and keys ricocheting across the room. Paige groaned and bent to grab her stuff. After she packed the bag up again, she stood up and tossed her hair behind her shoulder, clutching her keys. "I don't know, maybe you guys are just jealous."

"Jealous?" Piper spat back. This was too much. How could Paige really think they had any motive other than protecting her?

"That's right, you guys are jealous because I found a nice, successful *human* guy to be with," Paige replied.

Piper was stunned. How could Paige say something like that to her and Phoebe? She wouldn't give up Leo for all the human guys in the world, and she was sure Phoebe would say the same about Cole. Besides, she'd thought Paige loved Leo and Cole like brothers. How could she insult them all like that?

"I don't know what to say to you except we're telling you the truth," Phoebe said shakily. She was clearly as thrown by Paige's accusations as

Piper was. "We're your sisters, we care about you, and we're telling you the truth."

"Whatever," Paige said, shaking her head. "I'm outta here." She turned, grabbed her wrap from the couch, and stormed out of the attic.

"Where are you going?" Piper asked as she and Phoebe followed her to the top of the stairs.

"That's really none of your business," Paige shouted back. A few moments later they heard the front door slam, and then Paige's car sputtered to life outside.

Piper pulled in a breath to calm her frazzled nerves and pressed her hands into her forehead, unable to absorb exactly how badly that conversation had just gone. She clomped back into the attic, shaking her head. "That did not just happen," she said.

"What are we going to do?" Phoebe asked, her voice near panic as she placed *The Book of Shadows* back on its pedestal in front of the window. "Where do you think she went?"

"I don't know," Piper said, lowering herself onto the couch. She glanced at the door, wishing they'd done something to keep her there. "I just hope she doesn't do anything stupid."

Unfortunately, Piper knew that in the state Paige was in, there was a very good chance her sister was about to run headfirst into some serious trouble.

Chapter
7

Paige's pulse was pounding with anger and trepidation as she steered her car along the darkened, windy road that led to Micah's estate. Anger at her sisters for treating her like a child and for trying to take away the one guy she'd liked in ages. Trepidation over how Micah would receive her when she came knocking on his door just an hour after walking out on him. She gripped the steering wheel, watching carefully for landmarks on the side of the road. Having only been to Micah's house once, she wasn't entirely certain of where she was going and she hoped she wouldn't get lost. That was the last thing she needed after everything else that had happened that night.

"Thank you!" Paige said aloud when she saw an ornate mailbox she recognized.

Her nerves calmed the slightest bit once she

knew she was on the right road. The steeper
the hill became, the more her put-putting car
struggled, and by the time Paige got to the gates
outside Micah's house, she had her foot to the
floor just to keep the clunker running. She
pulled up next to the little silver box Micah had
used to enter the grounds earlier and put her car
into park. "Now what?" she whispered, glancing up at the very unwelcoming gates.

She looked at the box and noticed there was a
flat, circular button just next to the slot for
Micah's entry card. It was worth a shot. Maybe
there was a hidden microphone and speaker and
Micah would buzz her in just like at an apart-
ment building. She rolled down her window,
pressed the button, and waited for something to
happen. And waited. "Come on," Paige muttered, shivering in the rapidly cooling air.

Suddenly there was a quiet beeping noise,
and then the gates clanged open just as they had
earlier that night. Paige's heart hit her throat
at the unexpected noise, and for a moment she
didn't move. This was odd, wasn't it? With all
that security, why would Micah just have the
gates open when someone rang? Still, she wasn't
just going to sit there. She put the car in drive
and slammed on the gas, hoping to get her car to
make it up the last little hill to Micah's house.

A few minutes later, she pulled to a stop in
front of the mansion and took a deep breath.
"Just don't let him still be mad," she said quietly.

She climbed out of the car, dropping her keys into her purse, and looked up at the house. Micah was standing in the open front doorway.

"You came back," he said, grinning. He hadn't changed out of his suit, and Paige was certain she'd never seen a more welcoming sight in her life.

"I did," Paige replied with a small smile. "The emergency was apparently imaginary," she said, walking around the front of her car and up the few steps to the door. "I'm sorry about running out on you before," she said, smiling up at him. "It won't happen again."

"Oh, I don't doubt that," Micah said with a sexy smile.

He slipped his arm around her shoulders, and Paige relished the warmth the gesture afforded her. Together they strolled back into the mansion. Micah paused to close the door behind them, and locked it.

"How did you know it was me?" Paige asked as they walked through the foyer.

"At the gate?" Micah asked. "Security cameras."

"Wow. You really *are* Batman," Paige joked.

Micah smirked and squeezed her shoulder. "Something like that."

"So . . . how about that tour of the garden?" Paige asked, tilting her head to look up at him when they entered the library.

Micah's face positively lit up at the suggestion,

his blue eyes dancing. "I'm glad you asked," he said. He pulled away from her and took a long, black coat from a coatrack in the corner. Then he placed it over her shoulders and took her hand.

"Thank you," Paige said, touched by his gentlemanly manners.

Oh, yeah, he's a demon. Right, Paige thought sarcastically, pulling the warm coat closer to her as Micah opened the back door. She wished Piper and Phoebe could see them now—could see the way Micah treated her. She looked up at him and smiled as she stepped over the threshold onto the patio that bordered the garden. *I have nothing to worry about,* she thought. *Nothing at all.*

Micah closed the door behind them, and Paige took a few steps across the patio, expecting him to join her. When he didn't, she turned around to see where he'd gone. He was standing with his hand on the brass doorknob, his eyes closed and his head tipped forward. "Is everything okay?" Paige asked, concerned. He looked as if he may be ill.

But Micah raised his head, opened his eyes, and smiled. "Yes, I'm fine," he said, shaking off whatever it was. He walked over to her and took her hand. "I can't wait to give you the tour."

Paige smiled as they strolled off the patio and onto the grass. There was a small, gurgling fountain in the center of a square that was surrounded by perfectly trimmed hedges. Paige looked down into the clear water as they passed by and saw that the floor of the fountain was made up of tiny aqua blue tiles, each centered by a gold circle. The rippling water made the colors shift and twist in an almost mesmerizing dance. Micah tugged on her hand, and she followed him to the far end of the lawn and through a break in the hedge.

Her mouth opened in silent wonder as she took in the next garden. It was almost like walking from room to room in a house. This area was also bordered by the hedge, but it was much bigger and it was dotted with stone benches and flowering bushes more beautiful than any Paige had ever seen.

"What are these?" Paige asked, reaching out to cup the bulb of a fat red flower in her palm.

"That's a rose," Micah replied.

"No. It can't be," Paige said. She leaned forward to smell the flower and sure enough, it smelled just like a rose. "I had no idea they could grow so huge," she said.

"My gardener is a hybrid expert," Micah explained as they wove their way through the garden, admiring the other flowers. "These blooms are all genetically engineered. He's come up with some amazing things."

"It's incredible," Paige said. How was it possible that in addition to all of Micah's other amazing qualities, he was also a flower expert? *This guy could keep me in fresh-cut bouquets for the rest of my life.*

Micah walked her around the hedge at the end of the garden, and Paige was surprised to see a small, stone house, almost covered with flowering weeds, set back in the corner of another hedge wall. "What's that?" she asked.

"A supply shed, mostly," Micah said. "But there's also a powder room in there so that my guests don't have to walk all the way back to the house to use the facilities."

"Thoughtful touch," Paige said with a smile.

They came around another corner and left the hedges behind. The last garden was bordered by the brick wall that ran around all of Micah's grounds, but this garden was immense. There were huge trees growing along the wall to Paige's left, their gnarled roots pressing under the bricks and out the other side. In the far corner, a tiny man-made pond with a running waterfall was surrounded by another small, stone patio. Two chaise longues and a glass table with a retractable umbrella and four cushioned chairs were placed near the pond.

"I guess this is where you come to get that perfect tan of yours," Paige said.

"I don't have a lot of downtime, but when I do, this is where you'll find me," Micah replied.

"I think that a guy like you should make

more time for himself," Paige said lightly as they turned and walked back through the hedges and past the toolshed.

"Do you? For what?" Micah asked.

"For relaxing," Paige said, pulling away from him and sitting down on one of the stone benches in the flower garden. She raised her shoulders and blinked up at him flirtatiously. "For . . . patting yourself on the back for all your good works."

Micah laughed and sat down next to her, reaching up to brush a stray lock of hair away from her face. Paige's skin tingled at his touch and she could suddenly feel her heart beating as if it were the only thing in the world to feel.

"For . . . spending as much time as possible with your new girlfriend?" she said hopefully.

Micah leaned toward her, causing her pulse to race wildly, and reached over her shoulder to pluck a single red rose from the bush that grew next to the bench. He handed it to her, and she brought the beautiful flower slowly to her nose, gazing at him the whole time.

"That's the first good reason I've heard," he said, his voice deep.

Nearly trembling, Paige lowered the rose and Micah slipped his hand behind her neck, pulling her to him. Her eyes fluttered closed just before their lips met in a kiss like none other Paige had felt before. She felt it in her fingertips, her toes, her ears, her head, her heart. It seemed as if

Micah was wrapping her up in the warmth of his feelings for her and cradling her to him. By the time he finally released her, she was floating somewhere near the moon.

"Well? What do you think?" Micah asked, gazing down at her.

"About what?" Paige said, feeling almost drunk. She could barely open her eyes, and her head was swimming.

"About the garden," Micah asked, running his fingertips along her cheekbone.

"I think it's incredible," she replied, blinking a few times to try to knock herself out of her giddy trance. "I think I need to win the lottery so I can get myself a place just like this," she added.

"Sorry," Micah said. "It's one of a kind. But you are going to have plenty of time to enjoy it."

"Really? Does that mean you're definitely hoping to see me more often?" she asked coyly, smiling up at him.

"A lot more often," he responded, his blue eyes penetrating.

He leaned forward again and put his lips to Paige's forehead, giving her a firm, lingering kiss. Then he pulled away and smiled at her almost sadly. At that moment Paige suddenly knew that there was much more to Micah Grant than met the eye. He had secrets, just like everyone did, and she wanted more than anything to know everything about him.

He's seen so much sadness, Paige realized. *And*

*he's such a kind, giving person. How could Piper and
Phoebe ever have thought he was evil?*

Micah pressed his hands into his thighs and
stood, and Paige rose to follow him back into the
house. As enchanted as she was by the garden,
and as swept away as she was by Micah himself,
she was ready to get inside and away from the
cold. But she'd only taken one step when Micah
turned to her and held out his hand. "You have
to stay," he said firmly.

"What do you mean?" Paige asked, confused.
Was he going to get something and come back
outside?

"You have to stay," he repeated as if it were
the most normal thing in the world to say. "This
is your new home."

He turned and walked through the hedge wall
into the first garden, leaving Paige, who seemed to
be stunned frozen, behind. A chill more violent
than any she could have gotten from the cold
rushed over her. *What the hell is he talking about?*

Finally Paige was able to get her feet to move
and she rushed after Micah, her knees shaking.
When she came through the hedge, he was
already at the edge of the patio.

"Micah! What do you mean this is my new
home?" she blurted, still not quite able to believe
the words that were coming out of her own mouth.

He turned slowly and looked at her with a
patient expression, as if he was addressing
someone with only half a brain. "You're going to

stay here and be my love," he said matter-of-factly. "You said you loved my garden. And so, you'll stay in my garden."

Suddenly, every instinct in Paige's body was telling her to run. She could practically *hear* Piper and Phoebe screaming at her to get out of there as fast as her high heels could carry her. Micah was obviously not exactly sane.

"I'm going home now," Paige said firmly, her heart beating like a frightened bird's. She lifted her chin, trying to look unintimidated, and walked right past him. For a moment, she thought she was free. She thought he was just going to let her go. He certainly didn't make a move to stop her. But just as Paige was starting to feel as if she'd dodged one serious, heat-seeking bullet, the strangest, most disturbing, most incomprehensible thing happened.

She walked into a wall. A wall that wasn't there.

Steadying herself after being knocked back, and lifting her hand to an already-forming bump on her head, Paige looked around in confusion. No, she wasn't insane. There wasn't anything there. But she'd walked into something. She *knew* she had.

"What's going on?" she shouted, whirling on Micah as hot tears pricked at the corners of her eyes.

"I told you," he responded calmly. "You can't leave."

Panic seized Paige's heart and she turned toward the patio again, steeling herself. But when she took a step, she once again hit something solid. Something invisible, but solid. She reached out a trembling hand and felt the air, but it wasn't air at all. Her fingers felt as if they were running along a brick wall—a cold, grainy, completely impenetrable brick wall.

"No! This can't be happening!" Paige said under her breath. The bump on her forehead started to throb intensely. She had to get out of there before any more harm came to her.

Paige turned on her heel and ran for the side of the house, but Micah's brick wall—the real, visible one—ran right out from the corner of the mansion. It was at least ten feet high, and there was no way Paige could have climbed over it. Desperate, she stumbled along the wall, looking for an opening, but there was nothing. There was no way out.

Realizing she was actually trapped, that this nightmare was actually real, Paige turned and slowly walked back toward the patio, never taking her eyes off Micah. He simply stood there, hands in his pockets, watching her with a blank expression. His placid facade infuriated her.

"You can't do this to me," she said, struggling to keep the tears at bay. "You can't keep me here."

"It's for your own good," Micah said serenely. "For *our* own good." He took a step toward her, and Paige forced herself to stand her ground and

not back away. She didn't want him to know
how scared she was. Once he knew that, he'd
have even more of an upper hand, if that were
possible. "We were destined to be together
Paige. Soon, you'll grow to love me just as I have
grown to love you."

Paige was repulsed by the words that only
moments ago she would have been elated to
hear. For the first time she could see the coldness
in Micah's blue eyes. A steel-like coldness that
made her shiver beneath his thick, wool coat.
"You *are* Vandalus, aren't you?" she said
through her teeth. "You're the demon my sisters
warned me about."

Micah's face registered the same sorrow she'd
seen moments before and had attributed to his
deep, tortured soul. Paige had never felt so dis-
gusted with herself. How could she have been so
blind? He'd been planning this all along. He'd
been planning to keep her prisoner. No wonder
he'd been so hyped to get her into the garden.

"I'm hurt that you would think I am anything
but a man who loves you," Micah said.

Then he turned briskly and walked right
through the invisible wall and into the library.
Without giving herself a second to think, Paige
threw herself at the spot he'd moved through and
hit the wall so hard, she was tossed to the ground,
her shoulder throbbing with pain. She watched as
Micah walked over to the table in the library,
picked up her bag, and pulled out her cell phone.

"No," she said, scrambling to her feet. She pressed her hands up against the invisible wall desperately. "No!" she shouted.

She watched, her heart seized with helpless panic, as Micah brought the phone over to the glass door, placed it on the floor, and crushed it under his foot. His eyes never left hers.

"No!!!" Paige screamed, finally letting the tears spill over. "Don't do this! Micah! Please don't do this!"

But he simply turned away from her and switched off the light, leaving her in utter darkness, alone, cold, and with no hope of escape.

Chapter

8

Paige awoke the next morning to the sound of trilling birds and the soft, pink glow of the early-morning sky. She picked her head up from the cotton cover on the chaise longue in the back garden and a shot of white-hot pain blasted through her head. Tenderly, she touched the bump on her head and winced.

"That'll wake you up pretty quick," she said under her breath as she groggily looked around. Her eyes were heavy. They stung from the tears she'd shed the night before, and it took a moment for her to focus. But when she did, she knew that nothing had changed. She was still in Micah's garden. She was still alone. And no one knew where she was.

A breeze ruffled the leaves on the trees above and sent a cold shiver down Paige's back. She pulled the wool coat she'd used as a blanket tighter around her shoulders, curling up into a fetal position.

"Why is this happening to me?" she whispered hoarsely to herself. Her voice was nearly gone from hours of fruitless screaming the night before. A fat tear squeezed from her eye and rolled across her temple into the cushion as she felt more sobs welling up in her breast.

How could I have been so stupid? she thought, the tears coming more quickly. She'd fallen in love with a demon. A clearly *evil* demon. Not a hot and cuddly one like Cole. She was such a blind, silly little girl.

No! a voice in her mind called out. *You will not cry. You are not helpless. You're one of the Charmed Ones.*

Paige picked her head up again, ignoring the pain this time, and sniffled back the tears. It was daylight now, but it was still very early. Micah was most likely not up yet. If she was ever going to have a chance to escape, this was it. She stood and pushed her arms into the sleeves of the coat, wrapping it tightly around herself.

"Think you can hold me?" Paige muttered, glaring up at the house. "You don't know who you're messing with."

She walked over to the brick wall, took a deep breath, and closed her eyes. The night before, she'd tried to orb out of the garden, but hadn't even been able to move from one place to another inside the walls. She'd attributed the failure to sheer exhaustion and shock. But now she had to try again. She hadn't honed her skills enough to be able to orb herself all the way home, but she knew she was capable of getting herself past a single brick wall. "Okay. Here goes."

Paige concentrated and felt the whooshing, warm, pleasantly prickly feeling that engulfed her whenever she orbed. It was as if she were suddenly part of the air, part of the atmosphere. All she had to do now was envision herself appearing where she wanted to be. She pictured herself standing on grass on the other side of the wall. Saw herself making a run for it.

It's working, she thought, feeling her body dissipate further—feeling herself start to move.

But suddenly, before she'd even let the relief sink in, she felt as if she'd been thrust back to earth by a pair of rock-solid hands. Her feet hit the ground and she was whole again. Whole and still inside the garden walls. "The invisible wall must block magic," Paige whispered.

She felt the desperation start to build up inside of her again and she fought it back. After all, she wasn't just a Charmed One. She was also Paige Matthews—the girl who had sneaked out of her room countless times as a teenager and ditched school like a pro.

"There has to be some way out of here," Paige said, looking around. "Something he didn't think of." And if there was, she was going to find it.

"Paige?" Micah's voice called out, startling her. She whirled around to find Micah walking into the garden, smiling serenely as he carried a large tray filled with food. "I brought you some breakfast."

Paige's eyes narrowed as he walked by her and placed the tray on the table. The sight of him made a bilious taste rise up into her mouth. When he turned again to look at her, she pulled off his coat, trying not to visibly shiver as the cool morning air hit her bare arms.

"I don't want this," she said, handing it to him. "I don't want anything from you."

"That's too bad," Micah said, folding the coat over his arm. "I had the chef make some of his best dishes."

Suddenly the scent of pancakes, fresh bacon, and coffee filled Paige's nostrils. Her eyes flicked toward the table against her will and took a long look at the tray full of food, just beckoning to her angrily growling stomach. She forced herself to look away and refocus her gaze on Micah. "Forget it," she said venomously. "I'm not eating anything you give me."

A cloud seemed to pass over Micah's eyes, and his mouth set into a thin, determined line. "How else do you think you're going to get food?"

"I just won't eat," Paige said, straightening her shoulders.

Her stomach growled audibly, and Paige felt

a hot, angry blush heat her skin as Micah smirked at her. "I'm surprised at you, Paige," he said, turning to walk over to the table. "I thought you were smarter than this."

"Smarter than what?" she shot back, following him.

"You know there's no way out of here," he told her as he bent to pick up the tray. "And yet you seem resolved to make your life here as comfortless as possible."

Paige wanted to respond. She wracked her brain for something, anything, witty and biting, but there was no response. On some level, he was right. She was only punishing herself by giving up warmth and food. But she didn't want to give him the satisfaction of making her more comfortable.

"I've left some warm clothes for you," he said, turning his face toward one of the chaise longues. There was a pile of garments there—a pair of jeans, a cozy-looking sweater, socks, and sneakers.

"You can take those, too," Paige said, gazing steadily back at him. "Like I said, I don't want anything from you."

Micah drew in a long breath and let it out slowly, shaking his head. "I'm only doing this for your own good. I love you, Paige," he told her as he turned to go with the tray of piping hot food. "I wish you could see that."

He cast a glance at the clothes, then passed

them by, leaving them for her. Paige glared angrily after him, her eyes filling with tears. The clothes had been left to tempt her into accepting his help. Before she could change her mind, she picked them up in her arms and threw them as hard as she could into the pond, letting out a gutteral growl. "I hate you!" she screamed after him, hot tears streaming down her face. "I hate you for doing this to me!"

She sat down hard on the one of the chaises, her body wracked with sobs.

Maybe Piper and Phoebe will come save me, she thought sorrowfully. But she knew the chances were slim. After the way she'd stormed out the night before, her sisters probably just thought she was off somewhere, letting off steam, punishing them for thinking her boyfriend was a demon.

"Why didn't I listen to them?" Paige whispered through her sobs. "It's no wonder they treat me like a baby."

Phoebe pulled the SUV onto her block that afternoon, her pulse pounding with dread. She was barely able to focus on driving with all the thoughts in her mind fighting for her attention.

"Just let her car be there," she muttered. "Please just let her car be there."

But when she hit the brakes in front of the Manor, there was no sign of Paige's little red auto anywhere in sight. Phoebe killed the engine, grabbed her bag, and ran inside, her mind racing with horrifying possibilities. Paige could have gotten into a car accident, driving when she was as angry as she'd been the night before. She could have gone back to Micah's and he may have attacked her.

Or maybe she's just at work, she told herself, trying to be rational as she flung open the front door. *Maybe she just stayed somewhere last night and went straight to work this morning.*

"Paige?" Piper's terse voice called out the second Phoebe was through the door.

Piper rushed in from the kitchen, clutching the portable phone, and her face fell the moment she saw Phoebe.

"Still haven't heard from her, huh?" Phoebe asked, shrugging out of her jacket.

"Nope. And I've called her cell phone about a thousand times. Keep getting her voice mail," Piper replied. "Did shopping help you get your mind off things?"

"Do you *see* any bags?" Phoebe asked, thrusting her hands out at her sides. All she'd done for the past two hours was move numbly and blindly through her favorite stores, freaking people out with her zombielike behavior. She rubbed her forehead, the jittery feeling of foreboding in her gut growing stronger by the second. "Did you call her at work again?"

"Yeah, I got her voice mail there, too," Piper said, leaning back against the doorjamb between the foyer and the living room. "I tried the general number, and they said she could be out on a case this morning. She sometimes goes directly out into the field before she goes to the office."

"But you don't think she did that, do you?" Phoebe asked, hearing the skeptical vibe in her sister's voice.

"I hate to say it, but I'm officially worried," Piper said. "It seems like no one she knows has heard from her since last night."

Phoebe took in a shaky breath, almost afraid to suggest what she was about to suggest. "What about Micah?" she asked.

"Shockingly enough, the guy is unlisted," Piper replied with a sardonic smile.

The foreboding sensation kicked it up another notch and Phoebe suddenly felt that if she didn't do something quick, she was going to come right out of her skin. If Paige *was* with Micah, and if Micah was, in fact, Vandalus, he could be doing anything to her. *She may already be*— "Okay, that's it," Phoebe blurted, starting up the stairs and trying to block herself from further morbid thoughts. "I'm going to find out more about this guy."

"I'm right behind you," Piper said.

A few minutes later, Phoebe was sitting in front of her computer, staring at a long list of articles that had scrolled up when she'd typed Micah's name into an Internet search engine.

Piper walked back and forth behind Phoebe's desk chair, her arms crossed over her stomach.

"This guy is like a saint," Phoebe said, actually feeling disappointed. At least if they knew for sure that Micah was the enemy, they'd have someplace to start—someone to fight. "All he does is raise money for children's charities, open orphanages, lobby Congress, and schmooze celebrities for cash."

"I don't get it," Piper said, leaning her hands into the back of Phoebe's chair. "Where's the evil?"

"I don't know," Phoebe said, her eyes searching the screen. She clicked the mouse and scrolled down, past the many philanthropic articles and awards, and suddenly something caught her eye *and* made her heart catch. "Look at this," she said, highlighting the article. "Girl found dead in boyfriend's office."

"Scoot over," Piper said, sitting her butt down next to Phoebe's on the small chair and forcing her aside so that they were each half on the seat, half off. Phoebe braced her foot against the floor to keep her balance.

The article flashed onto the screen, and Phoebe's eyes widened. "'Well-known philanthropist Micah Grant is said to be "shocked and devastated" by the violent death of girlfriend Karen Carthage, found mutilated in his foundation's offices Saturday night. Carthage is the third woman tied to Grant who has lost her life in the last five years, but as of now, authorities say, Grant is not a suspect.'"

Phoebe looked at Piper, matching baffled expressions on both their faces.

"Three girls and he's not a suspect?" Piper said, raising her eyebrows. "Isn't there a little something called 'probable cause'?"

"'All three women have been killed by what officials deemed an attack by a wild animal,'" Phoebe continued reading.

"Sounds like our good friend Aplacum," Piper said flatly.

"'While the circumstances are bizarre, authorities have never been able to pin the deaths on Grant because he keeps no pets of any kind, and has never had a motive to kill,'" Phoebe finished. She leaned back in the chair, dumbfounded and more than a little disturbed. "We have to find Paige."

"Well, this is going to sound insane, but at least we know she's not going to be killed," Piper said, standing. "I mean, not in the same way these other girls died. We vanquished Aplacum. Unless some other wild animal was responsible for these girls deaths, Paige is safe from that."

"Okay," Phoebe said, willing to go with any and all positive thoughts. "But what's the deal? Why was Aplacum running around shredding all of Micah's girlfriends?"

Piper opened her mouth to respond, but

snapped it shut again quickly. "That, I couldn't tell you."

"I have to figure this out," Phoebe said, pushing her chair away from the desk and sweeping by Piper, heading out of the room. "We have to have missed something. If Micah *is* Vandalus, then what does he want with Paige? And why did Aplacum want all his girlfriends dead?"

She rushed to the attic stairs and took them two at a time, determined to read every single word about Aplacum and Vandalus in *The Book of Shadows* over again. She felt responsible for Paige and any danger she may have gotten herself into with Micah. After all, if it hadn't been for Phoebe's vision, they never would have encountered Micah in the first place. And if they hadn't encountered Micah, Paige would be sitting at her desk at work right now, safe and sound.

"Phoebe!" Piper called out as she entered the attic behind her. "Reading that again isn't going to help. You practically have it memorized already."

"I know, but I have to try," Phoebe said. "I have to—ow!" Phoebe swore under her breath and bent to pick up whatever the hard object was that she'd just stepped on. She snatched up a black crystal and laid it in her palm. "What is this?" she asked, holding the rock out to her sister.

Piper took one look at the crystal, and her face went ashen. Phoebe watched as her sister reached out a trembling hand and took the charm from her palm.

"It's . . . it's one of our protection crystals," she said, her voice thick. "Paige must have dropped it when she dropped her purse last night."

Phoebe swallowed hard. "Why is it black?" she asked, certain she didn't want to know the answer.

"It would only darken like this from fighting off some serious evil," Piper explained. "If she's had this every time she's been with Micah . . ."

"Oh, God," Phoebe said, bringing her chest just beneath her throat. She suddenly felt as if the world were crashing in all around her. "We have to scry for her, Piper. We have to find her—now."

Together, Phoebe and Piper ran down the stairs to the living room, where they kept their map of San Francisco and their scrying crystal. Using these tools, they could locate any witch or demon in the city. Sometimes scrying could be effective, but sometimes not. All Phoebe could do was hope that this time it would work right away.

"Here goes nothing," Piper said, raising the crystal on its chain over the map as Phoebe flattened the crinkly paper out. "Find Paige," Piper said, letting the crystal swing on its own over the winding, jagged streets of the city.

"Come on . . . come on . . . ," Phoebe said,

watching the crystal as it started to spin. Finally it dropped onto the map, and Phoebe and Piper both leaned in to see where it had fallen.

"That's it," Phoebe said. "That's the exact neighborhood where Micah's mansion is. It was in one of the articles." She turned and rushed for the door, grabbing her bag along the way. "Come on, Piper, let's go!" she said.

"I'm coming, I'm coming!" Piper said, pulling her leather jacket off one of the hooks by the door. "How are we going to find his house once we get into his neighborhood?" she asked as Phoebe opened the door for her.

Phoebe took a deep breath and sighed. "We're just going to have to hope for a little intuition," she said. "And a lot of luck."

Chapter
9

"This is it. This has to be it," Phoebe said as Piper pulled the SUV up in front of a huge, black iron gate at the dead end of an extremely steep hill.

"Why?" Piper asked, leaning forward and looking up at the gate through the windshield. "Why does this have to be it?"

"Just look at it!" Phoebe exclaimed, throwing her hand out toward the windshield. She popped open her car door and started to climb out. "This place just screams 'ancient evil demon.'" Phoebe pulled down on the hem of her denim jacket and slammed the car door, gazing up at the gates as if she was deciding just how high she'd have to jump in order to clear them.

That's exactly what she's doing, Piper realized with a start. She pulled the car over to the side of the road, away from the gates so it wouldn't be in plain sight, and turned the engine off. As she climbed out of the car and approached her sister, she had to admit that Phoebe had a point. The entryway was nothing if not foreboding, and there was an even more unwelcoming brick wall looming over her that seemed to run on for miles in either direction. Phoebe walked right up to the gates, wrapped her hands around the bars, and rattled them—hard.

"Phoebe!" Piper whispered through her teeth, her heart pounding against her rib cage. "Why don't you just announce that the cavalry is here?"

"Well, what do you suggest we do?" Phoebe asked.

"Come here," Piper ordered, waving Phoebe over to a more hidden spot next to the wall.

Phoebe rolled her eyes and clomped over to her sister. "Why don't you . . . you know . . . do your Matrix thing?" Piper suggested, pointing toward the sky.

"I was thinking about it, but that's only gonna get *me* in," Phoebe said, glancing up at the top of the wall. "If we really have a demon to face in there, we may need the Power of Three."

"True," Piper said. "But right now, I'm just concerned with finding out that Paige is safe. And if you get in there you can do a little reconnaissance, come back, and tell me what the deal is."

"Okay. Sounds like a plan," Phoebe said. She took a few steps back, still gazing skyward. Then she bent at the knees and launched herself into

the air, floating above Piper's head like a
Phoebe-shaped helium balloon.

"I will never get used to watching her do
this," Piper muttered to herself, tilting her head
back so she could see.

Phoebe arched slowly toward the wall, but
just as she was about to clear it, her arms and
legs splayed out and her face mashed up flat as
if she'd just hit a pane of glass. "Ouch," Phoebe
groaned.

Then, before Piper could even comprehend
what was happening, her sister was free-falling
through the air . . . coming down right on top of
her!

"Piper!" Phoebe called out, desperately claw-
ing the air with her hands.

Piper's first instinct was to jump out of
harm's way, but an instant later she realized
Phoebe would be better off with her there to
break her fall. She thrust out her arms, closed
her eyes, and hoped for the best. Phoebe hit her
like a sack of potatoes, and they both went
sprawling on the ground. Every inch of Piper's
body seemed to ache.

"Oh, God," Phoebe said, crawling away from
Piper. "Are you okay?"

Sitting up slowly, Piper moved her jaw back
and forth, feeling it crack. "I think you kicked
me in the face," she said, pushing her hair back
from her cheeks.

"What happened?" Phoebe asked, looking

skyward as she rubbed at her shoulder. "It felt like I hit the wall, but I couldn't have. I was above the wall . . . wasn't I?"

"As far as I could tell," Piper replied, tilting her head to one side and then rolling it back. "From this angle, you looked like something out of a Saturday morning cartoon. You know, like when the coyote tries to run through the rock after the road runner and he gets flattened."

Phoebe pushed herself to her feet and brushed the dirt from the back of her jeans. "There must be some kind of force field around the grounds," she said, slapping her hands together. "This is even more serious than we thought."

"All right, that's it," Piper said. She reached her hands up to her sister, and Phoebe grasped them both, pulling her up. "No more Missus Nice Witch," Piper said, stalking over to the gate. There was no way she was going to let her sister rot inside some demon's lair. Not if there was something she could do about it.

She lifted her hands and flung a burst of energy toward the gate, hoping to blow it to smithereens. Instead, there was a harmless pop as her power hit the force field and detonated itself uselessly. She may as well have thrown a firecracker at a missile silo. Disconcerted, Piper refocused her energy and tried again, with the same result. "We're screwed," she said, putting her hands on her hips.

"Not yet," Phoebe said. She grabbed Piper's arm and pulled her away from the gate. "Come on. Let's check this place out."

Piper followed her sister along the brick wall, looking for any sign of an opening, or any evidence that Paige had been there or had tried to escape. While obviously old and worn, the wall was nevertheless solid, and the longer they walked, trekking through bushes and high grass, the more helpless Piper felt. How could she have let this happen? She should never have let Paige walk out of the Manor the night before.

"We're never going to find her like this," Piper whispered, frustrated. "This place is like a netherworld Fort Knox."

"Wait! Shhh! Do you hear that?" Phoebe said, stopping suddenly and tilting her ear toward the sky.

Piper furrowed her brow, listening. "Hear what?" she whispered, placing her ear next to Phoebe's.

"Talking," Phoebe said, her eyes wide. "I think I hear Paige's voice."

Her heart took a wild leap, and Piper concentrated even harder. Sure enough, she heard the faintest of faint sounds coming from somewhere on the other side of the wall.

"Where is she?" Piper asked, pressing her hand into the jagged brick surface.

"I don't know," Phoebe answered. "Paige?!" she shouted. "Paige?! Are you in there?"

There was no answer. Phoebe started to walk faster along the wall, and Piper followed. Soon the voice began to grow louder and louder. She felt as if they were somehow getting closer to their sister, and the farther they walked, the more desperate she became for a glimpse of Paige. Piper had to find her sister and tell her that everything was going to be okay.

"Piper! There's a hole!" Phoebe whispered excitedly. She bent at the waist and stuffed her fingers into an indentation in the wall, digging out what appeared to be hundreds of years' worth of dirt and leaves. "I've got it! Look!" Phoebe exclaimed, running her fingers along the edge of the small square opening, about half the size of a brick, to get it as clean as possible. She leaned in close and peeked through the wall. "There she is! Piper! I can see her! She's okay!"

"Let me see," Piper said, jostling Phoebe aside.

She pressed her face up against the wall and saw Paige, lying back on a stone bench in the center of a beautiful garden. She was still wearing her gown from the night before, and her hair was knotted and matted in the back. She was staring up at the sky and she was, in fact, talking to no one. It sounded like she was reciting something from memory.

"Paige!" she stage-whispered.

Her sister lifted her head and looked around.

"Paige! Over here!"

Paige turned in her seat and scanned the walls, her eyes full of confused hope. Piper had no idea whether Micah was nearby or whether Paige was alone. The last thing she wanted was for Micah to catch them and do heaven knows what to them and to Paige, but she had to talk to her sister and find out what was going on.

"Over here! There's a hole in the wall!" Piper said a bit more loudly.

Finally, Paige's eyes locked with Piper's and she rushed over to the wall, falling to her knees so that she was level with the hole.

"Oh, thank God you're here!" Paige exclaimed, her eyes bright though her face was clearly exhausted. "Please tell me you're going to bust me out of this place. I'm so bored, I've been reduced to reciting movies from memory."

Piper smirked. Only Paige would think to complain of boredom while stuck in a potentially life-threatening situation.

"How did you guys find me?" Paige asked.

"Well, when we didn't hear from you all day, we decided to do a little research on Micah. . . . ," Piper explained. She trailed off and looked down at the ground, unsure of how much she should say. The information she and Phoebe had dug up on Micah wouldn't exactly be comforting to her sister in her present circumstance.

"What is it?" Paige asked, clearly trying to sound strong. "Piper, tell me."

Taking a deep breath, Piper looked her sister

in the eye. "In the last five years, three of his girl-friends have been murdered," she said.

"Oh, my God," Paige said, leaning back slightly.

"Tell her the good news!" Phoebe whispered, nudging Piper's shoulder.

"There's good news?" Paige asked.

"If you can call it that," Piper said flatly. "It seems that Aplacum actually killed the girls, so since we vanquished him—"

"I'm safe," Paige said. Then she snorted a laugh. "Sort of." She looked down at her hands. "Piper, I'm so sorry I didn't listen to you last night. You were right. I should have stayed away from him."

"It's okay," Piper said. "Don't worry about that now. Are you all right? Has he hurt you at all?"

"No. Not technically," Paige said, wrapping her arms around herself and glancing over her shoulder. "But I'm trapped and I'm hungry and I really don't want to spend another night out here. Please tell me you have a way to get me out."

Piper glanced at Phoebe, unsure of what to say. How was she supposed to tell her sister that the rescue squad couldn't even get past the front gate?

"Let me," Phoebe said, shooing Piper away from the hole. She knelt down in the dirt and smiled reassuringly at Paige. "Hey," she said.

"Phoebe. I'm so sorry," Paige said again, her voice breaking. The crack in Piper's heart deepened.

"It's okay," Phoebe said. "Now listen, why don't you try orbing out?"

"I did, a few times," Paige responded. "It doesn't work. He has this inviso-wall around the whole place and I can't get past it."

"What about Leo?" Phoebe asked, looking up at Piper. "Maybe he can get in there."

"It's worth a shot," Piper said. She could use some husbandly moral support right now, anyway. As strong as Piper was, she always felt a bit stronger when Leo was around. "Leo!" she hissed, looking at the sky. "Leo! We need you!"

Almost instantly, a shower of white light rained from the sky, and Piper's husband materialized at her side. She moved into him without even thinking about it, and he wrapped his arms around her. Piper clutched his button-down shirt with her fingers, hugging him hard.

"What's wrong?" he asked Phoebe, who was slowly standing up.

"It's Paige," Phoebe said. "She's stuck on the other side of that wall, and there's some kind of magical whoozy-whatsie keeping us out."

"Whoozy what?" Leo asked, looking to Piper for an explanation.

"An invisible wall. A force field. Whatever you want to call it," Piper said, pulling away and raising her shoulders. "Whatever it is, we can't get in, and *she* can't get out."

"Okay, I'll see what I can do," Leo said.

Piper took a step back as the white sparks of light swirled up to engulf him again. For a split second Piper was sure that it had worked and at any moment she would see Paige standing safely before her. But before she could blink, Leo was back again. Alone. Piper had never been so unhappy to see him in her life.

"It blocked me," he said, his face lined with worry. Piper's heart thumped painfully in her chest. This was not a good look, or a normal look for her husband. He was seriously worried.

"No!" Paige cried out from the other side of the wall. "How am I going to get out of here if *Leo* can't even get in?"

"*Talk to her,*" Leo mouthed to Phoebe, who gave him a quick nod.

As Phoebe hit the ground again to distract Paige, Leo nudged Piper farther away from the wall. Piper found that she was holding her breath, preparing herself for the worst. "What is it?" she asked Leo, her throat completely dry.

"It's not good," Leo said, glancing over his shoulder at the wall. "Only some serious evil could keep me from orbing to one of my charges when she's in trouble."

"Well, we think the guy who's holding her in there is actually this demon . . . Vandalus," Piper said, feeling as if she'd had all the energy

drained right out of her. "Have you heard of
him?"

"Vandalus. It sounds familiar," Leo said, narrowing his eyes. "I'm going to go check with the
Elders about this."

"What?" Piper asked, stopping him with a
hand against his arm. She hated the desperate
tone in her voice, but she couldn't help it. "What
are we supposed to do in the meantime?"

"Why don't you check *The Book of Shadows*?"
Leo suggested. "See if there's some spell in there
for breaking through enchanted boundaries."

"But we can't just leave her in there with the
demon!" Piper protested in a hoarse whisper.

"I promise I'll be back as soon as I can," Leo
said calmly. He leaned in and gave Piper a quick,
reassuring kiss. "We're going to figure this out,"
he added, squeezing her shoulders.

"Okay," Piper said. She looked at the ground,
feeling unable to watch him orb off again.

Once Leo was gone, Piper slowly walked
back over to the wall, dreading telling her sisters
what she had to tell them. Phoebe looked up as
she approached. She took one glance at Piper's
face, and all the color drained from her own.
"What did Leo say?" she asked.

Piper knelt down on the ground next to
Phoebe and brought her eyes to the hole in the
wall. "Paige?" she said. "Leo's gone up to ask
the Elders what to do," she said.

"He's gone?" Paige asked, her voice almost

shrill. "But he has to get me out of here."

"And he will. *We* will," Piper said. She placed her fingers inside the little hole and took a deep breath. "But Paige, we're gonna have to go home and consult *The Book of Shadows.*"

"What?" Phoebe and Paige both blurted at the same time.

"You can't leave me here," Paige said, sounding like a little girl in the middle of a nightmare. "Please, Piper, I can't stay here alone anymore. You don't understand."

"I know, sweetie, but you're just going to have to sit tight," Piper said. "You have to trust us. You know we'll be back for you, but there's nothing we can do here right now."

Phoebe bit her lip and laid her hand against the wall, turning her face toward it as if she could see Paige as well. "Piper's right, Paige. The only way we can help you is if we find a way to break you out of there, and the only way we can do that is if we go home and check the book."

Piper heard Paige pull in a long, soothing breath and blow it out again. "Okay, you're right," she said. "But you have to swear that you'll come back and get me out of here."

"I swear," Piper said firmly, trying to infuse her voice with as much confidence as possible. "I swear we're going to get you out of there."

She only wished she felt half as sure as she sounded.

Chapter
10

"I hate leaving her back there," Phoebe said, trying not to let her emotions get the best of her as she and Piper rushed along the wall back toward the front of the house. She felt as if there were a thousand invisible strings trying to pull her back to Paige's side. Phoebe had never heard Paige sound so desperate and afraid. And she hated the fact that there was nothing she could do to help her.

"She won't be there long," Piper said firmly as they neared the corner of the wall. "*The Book of Shadows* will have the answer. All we have to do is—"

Suddenly Piper stopped and pulled back, causing Phoebe to slam right into her from behind.

"You have to warn me when you're gonna do that," Phoebe hissed.

"I hear a car," Piper whispered back, holding

up a hand to tell Phoebe to wait. As if that was
going to happen. When Piper peeked her head
around the corner of the wall, Phoebe's face was
right at her shoulder. She watched, her heart racing, as the iron gates creaked open. It seemed to
take forever before they were wide enough to let
a vehicle through.

"Let's make a run for it," Phoebe suggested,
her adrenaline pumping. "If we go right now,
we can slip through the gates before they close."

"Are you crazy?" Piper said, turning her
head. "If we do that, he'll see us!"

"So? If we get inside and he comes after us, at
least we can get to Paige," Phoebe said quickly.
"And once we're together, we can vanquish him."

"We don't *have* a vanquishing spell," Piper
pointed out. "And you're not going to be able to
help Paige if you're dead. Besides, that invisible
wall probably doesn't disappear when the gates
open."

Before Phoebe could argue her point further,
Micah's little red convertible rolled through the
gates and out onto the street. The sight of his
face filled Phoebe with enough ire to kick his
sorry demon butt all the way back to Hell. She
took a step forward, but Piper's hand shot out
and grabbed her wrist, holding her back. Her
sister's touch seemed to bring her back to reality,
and she made herself stay where she was. Piper
was right: She wasn't going to be able to help
Paige if she got hurt. Or worse.

Phoebe held her breath as she watched Micah, waiting for him to glance to the right and spot their SUV. If he did, they'd be toast. But he didn't even look. He just turned the car left and headed down the hill.

"Now's our chance," Phoebe said, darting out from behind the wall.

"The gates are already closed!" Piper called after her.

"Not to get inside!" Phoebe shouted back, running for the SUV. "To follow him! Come on, Piper! Before he gets away!"

Piper ran over to the driver's side of the truck and jumped in, then gunned the engine. Phoebe braced her hands against the car's ceiling and the door as Piper raced down the winding street, full of blind spots and hidden driveways. There was never an open track of road long enough for them to spot his car—he was always at least one turn ahead of them.

"We're never going to catch him," Phoebe said, her heart falling.

"Oh yes we are," Piper shot back.

She slammed down on the gas, took a corner so fast that Phoebe was sure the left side tires actually came off the ground, and finally shot out onto the level stretch of road at the bottom of the hill. Phoebe felt a rush of relief the moment she spotted Micah's little sports car up ahead, stopped at a red light.

Pulling up behind him, Piper took a deep

breath and rested her elbow on the window frame. "So . . . why are we following him, exactly?" she asked. "Do you think he's just going to tell us how to break into his magical fortress?"

"No! But the more we know about him, the easier it'll be to find his weaknesses," Phoebe said, sliding down in her seat until she was hidden behind the dashboard. "Maybe we can figure out a way to bring him *and* his invisible wall down."

Piper looked down at Phoebe, her forehead wrinkled in confusion. "What are you doing?"

"You're right behind him!' Phoebe said, her chin tucked close to her chest as she curled up and rested her knees against the glove compartment. "If he looks in the rearview mirror and sees *one* brunette chick following him, he may not notice who you are, but if he sees *both* of us—"

"Good point," Piper said, slamming on the gas.

Phoebe looked up through her window, watching the streetlamps and electrical wires zooming past. It was all a little bit dizzying, and she had less than no idea where they were headed.

"What's he doing?" Phoebe asked Piper, who was the picture of determined concentration.

"I think he's stopping," Piper said. She hit the blinker and pulled the car up next to a curb. "Yeah. He's getting out. He's going into an office building."

"Let's go!" Phoebe said, ripping off her seat belt.

She scurried out of the car, Piper right at her heels, and walked down the sidewalk, trying not to look like she was a girl on a mission to save her sister's life. Piper pushed through a revolving door and Phoebe followed, but the second they were inside, Piper yanked Phoebe behind a huge potted tree. Phoebe glanced through the thick leaves and spotted Micah as he slipped into one of four elevators that opened up just behind a surly looking security guard.

The door to Micah's elevator closed, and Phoebe stepped out from behind the tree. The security guard stood behind his small desk and eyed Piper and Phoebe with moderate interest. From the marble and steel decor of the lobby, Phoebe could tell this guy probably saw nothing but business suits all day long.

"Hi!" Piper said brightly, approaching the guard. Phoebe kept an eye on the floor indicator above Micah's elevator as it climbed higher and higher. "We need to get upstairs," Piper said.

"To see who?" the security guard asked, crossing his arms over his chest.

"Piper," Phoebe said under her breath. "There's no one else in the lobby."

"All right, fine," Piper said. Just as the guard was registering curiosity, Piper flicked her wrists and froze him. "I hate doing that if I don't have to."

"Well, you had to," Phoebe said, grabbing her arm. "Come on. Micah stopped on the top floor."

Piper and Phoebe raced into a waiting elevator, and Phoebe pressed the button for the twentieth floor. Just before the doors slid closed, Piper threw her hands out once again, and the guard unfroze. Phoebe saw him look around, surprised that she and Piper had disappeared, and then the doors closed in front of her. "Come on . . . come on . . . ," Phoebe said impatiently as the elevator rose.

The doors finally opened up onto a posh floor, decorated in gleaming wood and earthy tones. A pretty, young receptionist smiled the moment they stepped out of the elevator.

"Can I help you?" she asked, folding her hands on her desk.

Phoebe glanced behind her at a closed office door. "Yes. Did Micah Grant just go in there?" she asked.

"Well, yes, he did," the receptionist said, blushing slightly. Clearly she had a little crush on their demon friend. "He's meeting with Mr. Reingold."

"Mr. Reingold?" Piper said. "As in Terrence Reingold, CEO of MicroCorp?"

Phoebe and Piper exchanged a glance. Terrence Reingold was San Francisco's richest man, and probably one of the top ten most powerful businessmen in the country. He had a reputation for being maniacal, egotistical, and seriously territorial about his riches.

Maybe he's in league with Micah, Phoebe thought, her heart thumping hard with foreboding.

"Yes," the receptionist said, a little crease forming above her nose. "These are his private offices. Do you have a meeting with Mr. Reingold? Because there's nothing on my schedule."

Phoebe tensed up. The woman was obviously starting to get suspicious. She glanced at Piper and pursed her lips, tilting her head toward the receptionist. Piper rolled her eyes, but she flicked her wrists and froze the room. The receptionist stopped with her hand halfway to the phone, undoubtedly to call security.

"We have five minutes," Piper said. She walked over to the office door and cracked it open ever so quietly. It opened up onto a sitting room, which was empty. But across the room was another door, this one slightly ajar, and there were voices coming from inside.

"Here goes nothing," Phoebe said, tiptoeing across the room.

Piper stood on one side of the door, out of sight, while Phoebe pressed her back up against the other side. She could hear everything perfectly.

"I need that money, Terrence," Micah said, sounding tense. "You promised me that money."

"Yes, I did," an older man's voice answered. His voice was quite calm and confident. "But I rethought it, and there's just no way. I don't know what I was thinking, telling you I'd donate to your *cause*." He said the last word with disdain. "Quite frankly, my corporation is not in the habit of throwing good money after bad."

"You will give me that money," Micah said.

Phoebe glanced at Piper, alarmed. Micah was starting to sound threatening. From the sound of the conversation, Reingold was not, in fact, in league with Micah. And, as bad as Reingold's reputation was, she wasn't going to let Micah hurt him. Moving as slowly as humanly possible, Phoebe peeked around the door. Piper waved her hands frantically, but Phoebe ignored her. She had to see what was going on.

Micah was leaning over Reingold, pressing his hands into the armrest on the older man's chair. Reingold stared back at him, resolved and almost amused. He clearly did not feel he was in any danger.

"You will give me that money," Micah said again, looking into Reingold's eyes.

Then, suddenly, the man's face lost all expression. His eyes were blank, as if he was hypnotized. Phoebe swallowed hard, a cold jolt of fear rushing through her heart. Had Micah put a spell on the guy just by looking at him? Who had that kind of power?

"Yes . . . yes, of course," Reingold said, sitting up straight. "Which account would you like me to transfer it to?"

"My personal account," Micah said with a smirk. He moved away to give Reingold enough space to sign on to his computer. "And one million dollars would be fine."

"Fine," Reingold said as he typed. "It's a pleasure doing business with you, Mr. Grant."

Micah started to look up and Phoebe jumped back. "*Let's go*," she mouthed to Piper.

Heart pounding, she led her sister back out to the receptionist, who was still frozen. They stood right where they'd been moments before and Piper unfroze her.

"You know what?" Phoebe said as the receptionist put her hand on the phone. "We must have the wrong floor. Sorry to bother you."

With that, she and Piper turned and fled for the stairs. The door closed behind them just as Micah emerged into the outer office. As far as Phoebe could tell, he hadn't seen them.

"What happened back there?" Piper asked as she and Phoebe started down the steps.

"He manipulated the guy . . . just by looking into his eyes," Phoebe said, still shaky from what she'd just witnessed. "Reingold was adamant about not giving him that money, and then Micah stared into his eyes and poof! 'Here's one million dollars.'"

"This is not good," Piper said, clomping down the stairs. "We're dealing with a guy who can cast invisible walls *and* mess with people's heads without breaking a sweat."

"I thought he was banished to Earth in *human* form," Phoebe said. "What's with the serious magical powers?"

"I don't know," Piper replied. "But now we know where he gets his millions."

Phoebe took a deep breath and tried to calm her fraying nerves. She didn't like this one bit. If Micah could get one of the most powerful men in the world to hand over a ton of money he didn't want to part with, she didn't even want to think about what he could make Paige do.

A few minutes later, the two girls walked back out into the late afternoon sunshine and Phoebe welcomed the soothing feeling of the sun on her face after the gray endlessness of the stairwell. But nothing could erase the palpable fear in the air between her and Piper.

"So, what do we do next?" Piper asked as they slowly made their way back to the SUV.

"I don't have a clue," Phoebe said, stopping next to the car and leaning back against the side door. "What does he want with Paige?" she asked as Piper leaned back next to her. "Why is he keeping her trapped up there?"

"I don't know. I just hope Leo gets back soon with some answers." Piper sighed and looked up at the bright blue sky. "Because, you know that thing you said about finding his weaknesses?"

"I know," Phoebe replied, her stomach twisting. "We haven't exactly found any."

Chapter

11

Paige sat on the edge of the chaise, watching the sun go down, feeling as if it were her life that was sinking before her eyes. The farther the sun descended, the more helpless and deserted she felt.

Come on, you guys, Paige thought. *Where are you?*

If Piper and Phoebe didn't come back for her soon, she was going to have to spend another long, cold, dark night out here by herself, not knowing what Micah wanted with her, wondering every second if he was going to hurt her.

The last bright sliver of the sun sank below the horizon, leaving the sky bathed in bright pink light. Paige sighed. It was the first time in her life that she hadn't been able to appreciate the beauty of a sunset.

Something must have gone wrong, she thought,

pulling her knees up under her chin. *What if Micah got to Piper and Phoebe? What if he did something to them?*

She wrapped her arms around her legs and clutched them as close to her body as she could. She hated this feeling. This feeling of not knowing what was going on outside of those impenetrable walls. Her sisters could be dead and she had no way of knowing.

Suddenly, Paige heard movement in the next garden and she sat up straight as Micah appeared, followed by an older male servant Paige had never seen. They were each carrying trays loaded down with silver-domed plates. Paige's stomach lurched, and she felt a wave of nausea so strong, she could barely make it to her feet. But she did. She didn't want Micah to see her curled up like a frightened child.

"I've had a lovely dinner made up for us, Paige," Micah said with a smile.

It was unbelievable how normal he seemed—how he didn't appear to realize what he had done to her—what he was doing. This was like any other date to him.

"Us?" Paige repeated, crossing her arms in front of her. Maybe if she clutched her stomach it would stop growling so much.

"Yes, us," Micah replied as he and the graying servant set their trays down on the table. Micah put his hands in the pockets of his freshly pressed khakis and waited until the man had

disappeared behind the hedge once again. "I see
you didn't like the clothes I brought you," he
said, casting an amused look at the fountain
where the clothes had finally become water-
soaked enough to sink to the bottom.

"I told you," Paige said, "I don't want anything from you."

Except that food, a little voice in her mind cried
out weakly. *I really, really, really want that food.*

"Hungry?" Micah asked, as if he had read her
mind.

Paige tore her eyes away from the steaming
trays, irritated that she'd let herself get caught
salivating. She sat down on the chaise again and
turned her back to the table. If she hadn't gotten
herself off her feet at that moment, there was a
good chance she would have fainted from
hunger. Every inch of her body was shaking,
and her heart was fluttering at an alarming rate.

"I'm not going to leave this for you, Paige,"
Micah said, his voice turning cold. "If you won't
eat with me, you won't eat at all."

"Fine," Paige said, firmly. "Then I won't eat."

She heard him sit down. Heard the chair
scrape back. Heard the little clinking sounds as
he lifted the covers off the trays. Delicious smells
hit Paige's nose at once, and she almost
swooned. Her mouth started to water as she
envisioned the meal being unveiled just behind
her. The clinking of silverware against ceramic
was more than she could take.

"You are unbelievable," Paige said, whirling on him. She glared at his face for a split second before the meal stole her attention. The plates were heaped with chicken in some sort of fragrant lemon sauce, pasta, bread, and salad. Paige couldn't remember a time when the sight of salad looked so appetizing.

"How so?" Micah asked archly, lifting a forkful of food to his mouth.

"I know about your other girlfriends," she said. "Did you imprison all of them here as well?"

"Those women didn't mean anything to me," Micah said matter-of-factly. He exhibited no surprise at the fact that she had this information. "You aren't jealous, are you? Because there's no reason to be. You're the only woman I love."

Paige didn't even bother trying to hide her shock and disgust. As if she cared about his past. As if she wanted the distinction of being his only love. If he'd said those words to her yesterday, she would have swooned, but today she could have spat in his face. So much had changed so very quickly.

"Why would I be jealous of a bunch of women who were murdered?" Paige demanded venomously. "You got all of them killed!"

Micah swallowed and braced his wrists on the table, setting his jaw as if he was trying to keep from losing his temper. "I didn't kill them, Paige. Aplacum did."

"Right, because of you," Paige spat back.

"That's enough," Micah said fiercely. He dropped his fork and his hand shot out, aimed at Paige. She flinched and clutched the cushion beneath her as a blast of heat sizzled past her face. There was a strange popping sound behind her, and Paige turned to find that the other chaise longue was gone. Just like that. He'd vaporized it.

Trembling inside, Paige slowly faced Micah again, trying to keep her body from betraying her fear. How could he possibly have such power?

I'm going to die here, Paige realized, swallowing hard. *If Piper and Phoebe don't come back soon, I'll never survive this.*

"I don't want to hurt you, Paige," Micah said, sternly. "But don't push me." He cut into his chicken casually, as if this were a normal dinner conversation they were having instead of an argument about the deaths of innocent people punctuated by the random annihilation of inanimate objects.

"You should take comfort in the fact that Aplacum is no longer an issue," Micah said as he took another bite. "You and your sisters took care of him for me. Now there's nothing standing in the way."

A thump of foreboding pounded inside Paige's chest. "Nothing standing in the way of what?" she asked, her hands curling into fists.

"In the way of you and me," Micah said,

fixing his cold blue eyes on her. "In the way of me and my destiny."

Paige's pulse raced as Micah continued to watch her. She knew an opportunity for information when she was handed one, but she had to play it just right. If Micah knew she was digging for information to relay to her sisters, he'd stop talking.

"Your destiny?" Paige repeated, rising slowly—carefully. She was seized by a blinding head rush, but she managed to steady herself and walk over to the table, never taking her eyes off his deadly hands. "How was Aplacum standing in the way of your destiny?" she asked, lowering herself into a chair. The food was so close now, she almost couldn't stand it. But by mustering all the strength she had, she managed to keep her gaze trained on Micah.

He eyed her carefully, obviously trying to discern her motives. For a moment, Paige was sure he was going to spill all, but then he turned back to his meal.

"All in good time," he said. "All in good time."

"What does your charity work have to do with all this?" Paige pressed on. "All those children you say you care so much about. Do they factor in, or are they just a cover?"

"A cover for what?" Micah asked flatly.

For your evil master plan, whatever it may be, Paige thought. But she wasn't about to say it.

That last blast of heat had come a bit to close to her face for comfort. "For this destiny," Paige said lightly.

"Oh, no," Micah replied with a chuckle, shaking his head as if her conjecture were ludicrous. "The children are part of it all. I'll need them when the time comes. There are thousands of them at this point—some grown, some still young. But I've made sure they love me. Made sure they need me. They are loyal. Where I lead, they will follow."

Paige's fists tightened as a cold, gripping cloak of fear enveloped her, tightening so quickly, she almost couldn't breathe. "Follow you where?" she asked, barely able to get the question out.

"Every general needs an army, Paige," Micah said with a smile. He looked her in the eye and blinked, then laid down his utensils. "I'm sorry, I can tell I'm confusing you," he added, his voice kind. "We can talk about this another time. Eventually, you will understand all."

Paige sat in silence for a few moments, her mind spinning. So it was true: Micah really was going to use those sweet little kids to execute his master plan, whatever it was. She knew from experience the affect Micah could have on a person—she'd thought she was in love with him after one date. Imagine the effect that charm would have on a little kid. But how was he going to make them into an army?

How, exactly, was he going to use them to bring about Hell on Earth?

She had a million questions to ask him, but she knew the conversation, in his mind, was over. She'd just have to bide her time and hope for another opportunity to find out what was really going on.

All she wanted at the moment was for him to get up and leave her alone so she could think. She glared at him, willing him to pick up his food and leave—to, at the very least, stop torturing her by continuing to eat in front of her. But Micah seemed to be engrossed in his meal, and with each passing second it became harder and harder for her to resist the food that was just inches away from her.

"Paige," Micah said, his voice throaty. "Look at me."

Possibly because she was so tired, possibly because she was so hungry, possibly because some irrational part of her still hoped there was some rational part of Micah in there, Paige did as she was told. The moment she looked directly into his eyes—his open, honest, deep blue eyes—a dizzying, heady feeling engulfed her. Her heart lightened, and everything that had happened in the past twenty-four hours seemed to melt away. There was only Paige and Micah. Micah and Paige.

Another head rush took over, clouding her vision, and a smile pulled at the corners of her mouth. Micah was so kind, really, to let her stay here. And he'd brought her this wonderful meal. Why was she turning it down? How could be so rude to this man who loved her?

"Eat something, Paige," Micah said, his voice sending a pleasant thrill over her skin. "I can't stand to see you like this."

"Well, maybe just a little salad," Paige said sheepishly, feeling silly for grandstanding as long as she had.

She picked up the fork in front of her and it slipped out of her hands, hitting the glass top of the table with a clatter. Paige's heart jumped, startled, and she blinked rapidly, her head suddenly clearing.

What is wrong with me? she thought, pushing the fork away. *Was I just having warm and fuzzy feelings for Micah?* She took a deep breath and tried to calm her beating heart. She was delirious from the hunger, that was all. She'd just have to be more careful from here on in.

"I'm not hungry," she said to Micah, narrowing her eyes.

"Paige, I just want you to be happy," Micah said.

"Save it," she shot back.

His face seemed to harden before her eyes, and her body seized up with fear. He was losing his patience with her. She was sure of it. Her eyes darted to his hands again. What would he do when his patience ran out entirely?

Micah took a sip of his water and paused before speaking again. "You should know that I'm aware your sisters were here today," he said in a bored tone.

Paige's heart dropped through her shoes. "H-how?" she asked, forgetting to play it cool.

"Security cameras, remember?" Micah said with a smirk. "I knew you three were witches, but those sisters of yours definitely have some serious powers." He looked her up and down in a way that made Paige shift uncomfortably in her chair. "What about you? What are your powers?" he asked, obviously intrigued.

"You'll never know," Paige said, looking away.

"Why haven't you used them against me?" Micah asked, sounding quite pleased with himself.

"Maybe I will," Paige replied, glancing at him out of the corner of her eye. She wasn't about to tell him that, alone, her powers didn't do her much good against him. There was no reason for him to know that.

"Well, I'll just have to watch my back then," he said with a laugh in his voice. "But what I want to know is, if your sisters are so powerful, why didn't they figure out a way to get you out of here today?"

Paige took a deep breath and focused her attention on the stone patio. She felt her eyes well up all over again and she hated herself for showing her weakness. But she *was* weak. She was exhausted and starving, and she couldn't keep up this strong act for much longer.

"You know what I think?" Micah asked, leaning in to the table. "I think they don't care about you quite as much as you'd like to believe."

Don't listen to him, Paige told herself, her grip tightening on her own arms. *He doesn't know what he's talking about. You can't give in to this despair or he'll have you right where he wants you.*

"I bet they tell you they care about you all the time, right?" Micah prodded, his voice seeming to touch every nerve in her body. "But that's not what's important Paige. Do they ever *show* you? Do they pay attention to your needs? The things really matter to you?"

No, the voice in her head responded like a reflex. *They don't listen. They don't care.*

She pressed her eyes closed and willed the voice away. That was just her despair talking. She couldn't let it get the best of her. Straightening up and rolling her shoulders back, Paige looked steadily into Micah's eyes. "You don't know what you're talking about," she said. "And I'd appreciate it if you'd take your disgusting food and get out of here."

Micah stopped smiling. He stopped chewing. He obviously was not used to being talked to this way and didn't like it. For a moment Paige thought she may have finally stepped over the line, but he simply rose from the table and placed his silverware down.

"Fine. If that's what you want," he said. He stood and deliberately covered each of the trays of food, leaving only the bread basket open, then turned toward the house and shouted out, "George!"

The elderly servant appeared in a flash, and Paige realized he'd been waiting on the other side of the hedge all along. He walked over to the table and picked up one of the trays, then allowed Micah to take the other and followed his master out.

Micah paused by the opening in the hedge and turned to Paige. "Good night," he said. "I hope you'll have come to your senses by the morning."

Paige said nothing, but when Micah had walked behind the hedge, she quickly lifted her hand and whispered, "Bread." The warm loaf disappeared from George's tray in a swirl of white light and reappeared in Paige's hand. The man didn't even notice, and in a breath, they were both gone.

Paige sat down on the chaise and hungrily tore into the bread, not even thinking about her earlier promise to herself not to eat anything Micah gave her. What he didn't know wouldn't hurt her cause, and she had to stay strong until Piper and Phoebe came back. They were going to need the Power of Three to fight Micah, and it was going to be more like the power of two and a half if she kept going without food.

The bread melted on Paige's tongue and she was sure she'd never tasted anything so delicious in her life.

Piper and Phoebe, Paige thought. *When* are *Piper and Phoebe coming back?*

The last thing she wanted to do was give any validity to Micah's accusations, but she couldn't help wondering if part of what he'd said was true. Her sisters had been neglecting the little things lately—tossing out her section of the paper, keeping her from using the car, blindly criticizing her boyfriend . . .

Okay, in that instance they'd turned out to be more than right, but still, did they have to disagree with her on every little thing?

"No, they love me," Paige said aloud, shaking her head to clear her thoughts. "They do. He's just trying to mess with my mind."

The sky was completely dark now, and Paige looked up at the stars, about to start her second night in captivity.

"But where are you guys?" she whispered uncertainly into the darkness. "If you love me so much, where are you?"

"There's nothing in here!" Piper shouted, slamming *The Book of Shadows* closed. It was all she could do to keep herself from throwing the priceless family relic across the room out of frustration. "How can there be nothing in there about magical force fields!?"

She walked away from the book, pushing her hands into her hair and holding it back from her face. It was already dark as pitch outside, and Paige was all alone. Who knew what Micah had done to her by now—what he might be doing to her at that very moment? What kind of sister was she if she couldn't help her? "I can't take this anymore, Phoebe," she said, her eyes prickling with tears. "I can't. She's right there and there's nothing we can do!"

She sat down on the rickety antique couch and rested her elbows on her thighs, still supporting her head as she gazed helplessly down at the floor. The longer she sat, the more it felt as if the musty room were closing in around her and all the oxygen was being sucked out of the atmosphere.

"It's gonna be okay," Phoebe said, sitting down next to her and wrapping her arm around Piper's back. "We're gonna get her back."

Piper looked up at the ceiling, trying to make herself breathe and keep the tears at bay. "Where is Leo?" she asked, her voice cracking. "What is taking him so long?"

At that moment, Leo orbed into the room right in front of them, but Piper's relief at the sight of her husband was short lived. She took one look at his face and felt as if someone had just pulled the couch out from under her. "What's wrong?" she asked, not sure she could take the answer.

"It doesn't look good," Leo said, not one to sugarcoat in times like these. "Micah *is* Vandalus and he is seriously bad."

"How seriously bad?" Phoebe asked, still holding on to Piper.

"We're talking Armageddon time if he regains full power," Leo replied, looking them each in the eye.

"Yeah. We had a feeling," Piper said, pushing herself to her feet. "We saw Micah do his little thing today."

"His little thing?" Leo repeated, his forehead creasing.

"Yeah. If you call looking into a person's eyes and making him part with a million dollars a little thing," Phoebe explained. She leaned against the arm of the couch, looking pale. Piper knew that her sister was seeing the scene at Reingold's office all over again.

"How do we stop him, Leo?" Piper asked. "He's supposed to be human and he has more power than the three of us combined. He can make anyone do anything."

Leo paced over to the window, his hand on his chin. "It makes sense that he has *some* power," he said thoughtfully. "He's been on Earth for so long, and a demon like that is going to figure out ways to regain strength."

"But the question is, what does he want with Paige?" Phoebe asked. "If he wanted to kill her he could have done that a million times over by now."

"Well, that's the really scary thing," Leo said, turning to look at them again. "Micah won't be able to become Vandalus again unless he gets one, small thing."

Piper's face screwed up with wary disgust. "I'm afraid to ask," she said.

"It's a kiss," Leo said. "A kiss of true love."

"A kiss?" Piper repeated, baffled. Then realization swept over her like a cold wind. "That's why Aplacum killed all those girls . . . and wanted to kill Regina. As long as Micah didn't get his kiss of true love, Aplacum had no other demon to challenge him."

"Exactly," Leo said.

"But . . . Regina and Micah have kissed plenty of times," Phoebe said, leaning forward on the couch. "Why didn't she release the demon within?"

"The Elders told me that Micah has kissed scores of women in the past," Leo explained. "And a lot of these women have loved him . . . or at least *thought* they did. But somehow, it's never worked."

"How frustrating for the poor little demon," Piper said sarcastically.

"But the Elders think that if he could get a Charmed One to fall in love with him, the power of her kiss might be enough to set Vandalus free," Leo said.

Piper's insides twisted into tight, angry knots. "So he's going to use Paige to become this demon and basically take over the world," she said, an icy rush of fear racing down her spine.

"Well, then, we have no problem!" Phoebe said happily, tossing her long brown hair over her shoulder as she practically jumped off the couch.

"Delusional much?" Piper asked, raising her eyebrows. "How is this not a problem?"

"*Because,*" Phoebe said, rolling her eyes at her sister's obliviousness. "Paige is never going to kiss the evil demon that imprisoned her, let alone fall in love with him."

"Except . . . ," Leo said, grimacing.

"Except, all he has to do is look into her eyes . . . ," Piper pointed out.

All the color rushed out of Phoebe's face. "Oh, God."

"Exactly," Leo said, folding his hands together. "That's how he got so many girls to fall in love with him. The longer Paige is left alone with him, the harder it's going to be for her to withstand it—especially if she doesn't know it's coming."

"Piper," Phoebe said, her voice filled with fear.

Hearing it was almost more than Piper could bear. "We have to get her out of there," she said. "We have to find a way. *Now.*"

Chapter

12

Paige lay back on one of the stone benches in the flower garden, letting the warm sun push away the chill that seemed to cling to her after another night of shivering under the stars. She'd barely slept, thinking about her sisters, wondering where they were, listening for them at the garden wall. She'd passed out next to the hole in the bricks, her back up against the cold, grainy surface of the barrier. They hadn't come, and Paige had awoken with a painful knot in her back and an even more painful one in her heart.

"They're not coming back," she whispered, trying to make herself accept the truth.

If her sisters were really worried about her— if they really cared about her safety—they would have at least come back by now to check on her. Even if they hadn't come up with a way to break her free, they knew they could communicate with her. So why didn't they?

"Because they *don't* care," Paige told herself, the knot in her heart tightening painfully. "Micah was right. This is my life now. I'm going to spend the rest of my life in this grungy gown, sneaking food and being bored into insanity." She'd only been imprisoned for a day and a half, but with nothing to do and no one to talk to, it felt ten times as long

A pair of birds soared overhead, chasing each other against the clear blue sky. Paige smiled sadly. It was okay, really. At least her surroundings were beautiful and open and bright. He hadn't locked her in some wet, dank dungeon. *I've got to give Micah that much.*

"Paige?"

She sat up, startled, and waited for the now familiar head rush to pass. Micah had appeared silently at her side. He was holding a shopping bag and smiling down at her. The sun lit him from behind, causing a warm glow to surround him and making him look like an angel.

Right. A demon angel, Paige thought, smirking. Then a nagging feeling started to itch at the back of her mind and she watched him, waiting for a spark of recognition. He'd told her something the day before. Something important. Something she should remember. But it was gone. Whatever it was, it was long gone.

It doesn't matter anyway, Paige thought,

detached. *Even if I had information on him, it's not like there's anything I could do with it.*

"I brought you some things to . . . make you more comfortable," Micah said, sitting next to her almost tentatively.

Paige knew he was waiting for her to reject him again, but she didn't have it in her anymore. She wasn't afraid of him now. Seeing him inspired no feeling whatsoever, actually. Maybe this was part of her new life as well—not being able to feel.

He set the large bag at his feet and pulled out a few leather-bound books. Paige's heart leaped. Apparently she *could* still feel something: total relief. He may as well have been handing her a life preserver. She snatched the books out of his hand and flipped them over so she could read their spines.

"Austen . . . James . . . Brontë . . . Cather," she read, her eyes widening with each name.

Opening the cover of *Sense and Sensibility*, Paige ran her hand over the first page. She couldn't wait to lose herself in the stories. Anything would be better than sitting here all day and all night, thinking . . . slowly realizing that no one was coming for her.

"You like them?" Micah asked, his eyes brightening. "I remembered that on our first date you mentioned some of those authors, but I wasn't sure which books you'd like."

Paige piled the tomes on her lap and looked at Micah. His eyes were so full of hope, she was reminded of the qualities she'd first seen in him—of the romance and magic of their first date. And bringing these books to her was so thoughtful. He knew she needed a distraction. Even though he was keeping her here against her will, he was still thinking of her on some level.

Unlike her sisters, who seemed to have forgotten that she existed.

"Thank you," she said.

Micah smiled broadly, and Paige felt her heart skip.

Come on girl, keep it together, she told herself. *This is still the guy who's keeping you captive. The demon who's keeping you captive.*

"And I brought you these," Micah said. Reaching into the bag again, he pulled out a sweatshirt, sweatpants, socks, and another new pair of sneakers. "When I came over to your house that day, you were wearing sweats. I thought you might like them better than the things I brought you yesterday."

Paige reached for the sweatshirt and ran her hand along the inside of the fabric. The feel of the cozy fleece sent goose bumps all over her bare arms.

I could be so comfortable, she thought, looking down at her flimsy dress. *Why am I punishing myself like this? Who knows how long I'll be here? Maybe forever . . .*

"One more thing," Micah said. This time he

pulled a plastic box out of the bag and laid it on the bench between them. He opened it to reveal a bar of soap, small bottles of shampoo and conditioner, toothpaste, a toothbrush, and a hairbrush. "You've probably noticed there's a stall shower in the bathroom," he said.

Paige reached out and picked up the soap, her hand visibly shaking. She couldn't believe how grateful she was for something as simple as soap—something she'd completely taken for granted every day of her life. Suddenly she was hit with the realization of exactly how good it would feel to take a shower— to wash the grime of the last few days from her for good—and climb into these warm, clean clothes.

Don't do it, a little voice in her head warned. *Don't let him do anything for you.*

But while her survival instinct was loud, her need to stop smelling herself was louder.

"Thank you, Micah," she said. She placed her books aside and picked up the shower things and the new clothes. "I'm gonna . . . go," she said, tilting her head toward the next garden where the toolshed and bathroom were.

Micah's expression was elated as he rose to his feet. "When you're done, I'll have breakfast waiting."

Paige made herself smile, then walked off toward the shower, clutching her new things to her chest. She knew she should still be thinking about escaping. She should still be trying to remember whatever it was he'd told her the day before—something about his . . . destiny? But at that moment, all she could think about was the sensation of hot water hitting her skin, and ponder whether or not Micah's cook would make pancakes two days in a row.

"This food is so amazing," Paige said, taking another bite of French toast and savoring the sweet taste. So it wasn't pancakes, but it was just as good. "It's amazing that you're not the size of a house with a cook like this working in your kitchen."

Micah smiled at her and she blushed, realizing she was babbling. Babbling to her captor. But she couldn't help it. Ever since her shower—the longest she'd taken since she was a teenager who'd perpetually used up all the hot water— she'd felt lighter. Almost happy. She was clean. She was warm. And now she was full. These new comforts were all mixing together to create some kind of uncontrollable euphoria.

"Would you like to go for a walk with me?" Micah asked, sitting forward in his chair.

Part of Paige knew she should say no. He shouldn't be rewarded for treating her humanely— especially when he was holding her prisoner. But there it was again—that unabashed hope in his eyes. And it made her want to give him what he wanted. Besides, it was just a walk. "Sure," she said quietly.

She pushed her chair back and came around

the table. Micah reached for her hand, and a chill
of trepidation rushed through Paige's heart. As
grateful as she was for the food and the clothes
and the shower and the books, she wasn't
exactly ready to touch him. Instead, she tucked
her hands into the pocket on the front of her
sweatshirt. Micah's face registered disappointment, but he said nothing. He simply held his
hands behind his back and started walking.

"I'm so glad you're here, Paige," he said,
looking off into the distance as they traversed
the garden. "You have no idea how lonely it is,
living here all by myself."

Paige watched her feet as she walked. She
knew what it was like to be alone—and not just
for the past couple of days. Her adoptive parents
had died in a car crash when she was in high
school, and she had quickly learned what loneli-
ness truly felt like. But she wasn't about to open
up about it. Not to Micah. Not yet.

"I know you think I'm . . . evil," he said with a
disbelieving laugh. "But it's not that simple. You
have to know, living the life that you do, that
nothing is black and white."

They came through the hedge into the flower
garden, which, in the morning light, seemed to
be exploding with color. Paige paused by the
opening in the hedge as Micah walked over to
one of the rosebushes. She watched him as he
delicately touched one of the flowers, gazing at
it with loving admiration.

Paige did know about all the shades of gray of the universe. Sometimes rules were made to be broken. Sometimes questionable things needed to be done to bring about the right results. And people weren't always what they seemed. Take Cole, for example. He was able to fight against his demon side. He was a good person even though the demon Balthazar lurked somewhere beneath the surface, ready and more than willing to show his evil face.

If Cole could fight his demon nature, why couldn't Micah? Maybe that was why he was holding her here. Because he needed the time to show her who he really was and he knew that she wouldn't listen to him otherwise. Paige didn't think that kidnapping her was the right thing to do, but suddenly she could see why he had resorted to it.

Micah returned to her, carrying the most beautiful flower she'd ever seen: a lily so purely white, it seemed unearthly.

"I just want someone to love me for who I really am, Paige," Micah said as she took the flower gingerly from his fingers, her heart pounding. "The first moment I saw you, I knew you could be that person."

Paige brought the flower to her nose and took in a deep breath of its heady scent. When she looked up at Micah through her thick lashes, she felt as if she were seeing him for the first time. He was so handsome, so open, so cultured, so caring. Maybe he was part demon, but he couldn't be all bad. *How could anyone so perfect be all bad?* she thought.

A light breeze ruffled her hair, tossing a few strands against her cheek. Micah, looking unwaveringly into her eyes, reached up his hand and brushed it away from her face. His fingertips lightly grazed Paige's cheek as he tucked her hair behind her ear.

Paige didn't even flinch.

"I'm going back over there," Piper said, grabbing her car keys off the table near the front door of the Manor. She pulled her jacket off the hook and started out the door as Leo and Phoebe barreled down the stairs behind her.

"Piper, what do you think you're going to do when you get there?" Phoebe asked, out of breath. "You know you can't get past his barrier."

Piper's frustration was becoming unbearable. "I know that!" she shouted as she whirled around at Phoebe. "But I can't just leave her alone there anymore. I have to see if she's okay."

She clenched her hands into fists, trying to keep herself from using her powers to blow up one of the glass doors that lead to the parlor. Destruction was no way to vent her frustration, but it would feel so good.

"Okay, I know you're upset," Phoebe said, carefully approaching her sister. "But we need a plan here. If what Leo said is true, we're running out of time."

Piper looked from Phoebe to Leo, both of whom were gazing at her expectantly. It was clear that they were both waiting for her to come up with the plan. And why not? One of the burdens of being the oldest was being the one with all the answers. But this time, she was at a loss. This time she needed someone to take care of *her*—to tell *her* what to do. Because when it came to Paige, she couldn't think straight. Paige was her baby sister, and she'd just come into their lives, and now she was in danger—and it was all because of Piper.

"I shouldn't have let her go on Monday night, Phoebe," she said tearfully. "Or I should have looked at her protection crystal. She shouldn't be trapped like this."

"It's okay," Phoebe said, reaching out and hugging Piper. Piper clutched her back, holding on for dear life. When Phoebe pulled away, her face was the picture of determination. "I'm going to come up with a spell to take that wall down. And if I can't, we'll figure out another way. In the meantime, you're right: Someone should go check on Paige."

Piper nodded as Phoebe turned to look at Leo. "Why don't you take her there?" she suggested. "I'm going to get to work."

"Okay," Leo said. He walked over to Piper, wrapped his strong arms around her, and kissed the top of her head. "Just hurry," he said to Phoebe. "We'll be back soon."

Piper pressed her cheek against his chest and

let herself go as she was wrapped up in the warmth of his white light. A split second later they had materialized, in the exact same pose, just outside the brick wall at Micah's mansion.

Looking around, Piper spotted the hole Phoebe had made in the wall and crouched down. Paige was nowhere in sight, and Piper was instantly seized with fear. "Paige?" she called out desperately. "Paige! Where are you!?"

There was no answer. No movement. Piper looked up at Leo. "She's not there," she said, starting to panic.

"Piper, she could be anywhere on the grounds," Leo said, placing his hands on her shoulders. "Just keep trying."

"Paige!" Piper shouted. "It's Piper! Are you there?!"

Finally, Paige wandered into the garden, and Piper's heart skipped a beat. She looked okay. She looked . . . serene, in fact. Paige glanced over at the hole in the wall and walked toward Piper ever so slowly. Piper pressed herself closer to the opening, realizing something was wrong. She'd expected Paige to run to her like she had the day before, but her sister didn't even seem to be sur-prised—or all that happy—to see her.

"Hey, Piper," Paige said, lowering herself to her knees.

"Are you all right?" Piper asked. From the detached tone in Paige's voice, she could have been answering the phone.

"Sure," Paige said with a shrug as she toyed absently with the hood strings on her blue sweatshirt. The calm, detached expression on Paige's face was a far cry from the terrified vibe she'd given off the day before. Today, Piper couldn't help but think that her sister looked almost . . . content.

Piper narrowed her eyes as she watched Paige's hands. "Paige? Where did you get those clothes?" she demanded.

"These? Micah gave them to me," Paige said, looking down at her sweatshirt. "They're so comfy. He's been really sweet, Piper, bringing me books, making my favorite foods, picking me flowers . . ."

He's already gotten to her, Piper thought, her stomach lurching. *She thinks he actually cares about her. And if he's gotten that far, it won't take much more for him to get her to fall in love.*

"What do I do?" Piper mouthed to Leo.

"Try to snap her out of it," Leo mouthed back.

"Paige, sweetie, listen to me—you can't trust Micah," Piper said desperately, pressing both hands against the wall. "He's working some kind of . . . demon mojo on you. He's making you think you love him, but you don't."

"Why didn't you come back for me last night?" Paige asked simply, not looking the least bit interested in the answer.

"Paige—"

"Actually, you don't have to explain, Piper," she continued. "I know you have a lot on your plate. You've got Leo and the club and your real sister, Phoebe. I understand why breaking me out of here wouldn't be your first priority."

Piper's throat went dry, and it took a moment for her to find her voice. Was this the way Paige really felt, or was this just Micah's spell talking? "Paige, please listen to me," she said. "Micah has this power—"

"I know, I know," Paige said, rolling her eyes. "Micah is an evil demon, blah, blah, blah. But you don't know him, Piper. Not like I do. I see the good in him. He's compassionate, romantic, caring. He's not evil, Piper. He can't be."

Piper's head tipped forward, and she rested her forehead against the wall. This couldn't be happening. Paige could not really be falling for that evil bastard. *What is he doing to her?*

"Say something," Leo whispered, crouching next to Piper. "Anything."

"Paige, this isn't real," Piper said, her voice cracking. "You have to fight it. Micah's only using you so he can become Vandalus again. He's evil, Paige."

Paige scoffed. "Do you even hear yourself?" she said. "'He's evil, Paige.' Right. All Micah wants is to be with me. And that's more than I can say for you and Phoebe."

Her words cut through Piper. "Paige, you don't mean that. You can't—"

But Paige was already standing. Suddenly, Piper was looking at her sister's leg instead of her eyes. "I have to go now," Paige said, her voice muffled and distant. "It's almost time for dinner and I want to look nice for Micah. He's taking such good care of me—"

"Paige!" Piper shouted, putting her mouth right next to the small hole. "Paige! Don't go!"

Looking through the opening again, Piper saw her sister walking farther and farther away, across the garden. As much as she shouted, as pleading as her voice became, Paige never once looked back. When her sister finally disappeared through the hedge, Piper turned and sat down hard on the ground, her back up against the wall. "We've lost her, Leo," she said, her voice disbelieving. "We've actually lost her."

Chapter

13

Phoebe ripped the top page from her notebook, crumpled it into a tight ball, slammed it back and forth from palm to palm for good measure, and launched it across the room with a groan. She hadn't felt so much like a frustrated student since the day before her last final in college, but writing spells wasn't easy. Especially when her sister's freedom—her very life—might depend on it.

"Okay, concentrate. You've only done this a million times," she said aloud, pushing herself against the back of the couch and uncrossing her legs. A lock of hair fell from her French braid, tickling her cheek, and she tucked it behind her ear. She pulled the notebook into her lap, poised her pen above the page, and bit her lip. It was work time.

"Let's see . . . walls . . . locks . . . unlocking the walls . . ." Phoebe squinted up at the ceiling, flipping through the dictionary in her brain. "What rhymes with walls . . .?"

Suddenly a rain of white light sparkled down from the ether and Phoebe jumped, startled out of her concentration. Piper and Leo materialized in front of the couch, and Phoebe felt her scalp tingle the second she saw her sister. "What is it? What's wrong?" Phoebe asked, holding her breath.

"He's started to work his little spell o' love," Piper said sarcastically, kicking one of Phoebe's discarded paper balls across the room. She lowered herself into the chair across from the couch where Phoebe was perched and rested her head in her hands, pushing her fingers into her hair at her temples. "Paige was not acting like herself, let's just put it that way."

Phoebe swallowed hard and looked down at the mess she'd made of the living room. The entirely unfruitful mess. There were so many little white paper balls littering the floor, the hard wood was barely visible beneath them.

"Have you come up with anything?" Leo asked Phoebe, his brow creased with concern.

"I hate to say it, but no," Phoebe replied, fear mounting in her breast like bricks being laid in a new wall. "It's like I'm blocked or something, and I think I know why. I mean, if Leo can't get past that wall, is a spell really going to work? Especially when it's just the two of us?"

"Well, we have to try it," Piper said, sitting up straight. "What other choice do we have?"

"I may have an idea," Leo said, holding one elbow with his hand and bringing the other hand to his chin.

"We'll take it, whatever it is," Phoebe said. She shifted in her seat to better see him, pulling one leg up on the cushion and turning sideways on the couch.

"What about Cole?" he asked, looking Phoebe in the eye.

"What *about* Cole?" Phoebe asked, her pulse racing at the mere sound of his name. She hadn't seen him or heard from him in days, and she would have loved to have an excuse to get him in on Paige's rescue. She could use all the moral support she could gather right about now.

"Well, his power to shift from one place to another comes from evil," Leo said, causing Phoebe to squirm uncomfortably. Whenever her boyfriend was mentioned in the same sentence as the word "evil," she tried her best to ignore it. "I'm sorry, Phoebe," Leo said, his blue eyes sincere. "But that fact could really help us in this situation."

Piper rose slowly and took a few steps away from the chair. "Because his power to shift comes from . . . you know," she said, casting an apologetic look at Phoebe. "He may be able to pass through an evil barrier."

Phobe's heart took a few extra beats as she understood what they were saying. "Cole may be able to get inside," she said. "He may be able to get us all inside."

"It's worth a shot," Leo pointed out.

"Let's get him." Piper said.

Phoebe didn't have to be asked twice. She launched herself off the couch and clasped hands with Piper. "Calling spell?" she said, raising her eyebrows. Piper nodded, and Phoebe tightened her grip on her sister's hand. This had to work. She just hoped Cole was able to answer their call and return to the Manor safely.

"Powers That Be, return Cole to me," Phoebe and Piper recited together.

Instantly, the air in the room seemed to grow hotter and a transparent ripple appeared just before the two sisters. In a flash, Cole was there—shirt ripped, eye blackened, and obviously disoriented. He tipped forward weakly and reached out a hand to brace himself before he hit the floor.

"Cole?" Phoebe cried, crouching to her knees next to him and wrapping one arm around his body to steady him. "Are you all right?"

"Yeah," Cole whispered harshly. He was sweating and struggling to breathe normally. "You just pulled me out of a serious fight."

"Who was winning?" Leo asked.

Cole looked up at him, and Phoebe was relieved to see the usual cocky playfulness in Cole's eyes. "I was, of course," he said, standing and brushing himself off. "I like to let them feel they're doing their job before I finish them off."

"I wish you wouldn't joke like that," Phoebe

said morosely. "You're out there fighting for your life against God knows what and then you come back looking like this—"

"I'm sorry, Phoebe. I'm fine," Cole said, planting a kiss on her forehead. His simple touch was as soothing to her as a warm bath. Then he pulled back and searched her face, clearly worried. "Why did you call me back?"

"It's Paige," Piper said from across the room. "She's been kidnapped by Vandalus, and we may need your help to get her out."

"Vandalus?" Cole repeated, his face going slack. "Vandalus has Paige? For how long?"

"A couple of days," Leo said flatly.

"Why didn't you call me sooner?" Cole demanded, leveling each of them with an accusing gaze.

"You've heard of him?" Phoebe asked shakily, resting her hands flat on Cole's chest as she gazed up at him. "What do you know?"

"Enough to know that we have to get her away from him right now." Cole reached up and took one of Phoebe's hands in his own. "Where are they?"

"It's 135 Mercer Street," Piper said, crossing the room to Leo. "We'll meet you outside the wall."

"Wait!" Phoebe said. She reached out to the couch and grabbed the piece of paper that held her one success of the afternoon. "Vanquishing spell," she explained.

"Wouldn't want to forget that," Piper said through her teeth.

As Leo's white light enveloped him and Piper, Phoebe leaned into Cole's chest, saying a silent prayer that he would be able to get them through Micah's invisible wall. She had one last thought before she and Cole winked out of the living room.

Just don't let us be too late.

Paige couldn't believe her eyes when she walked into her small bathroom to get ready for dinner with Micah. Hanging on the far wall was the most beautiful ball gown she had ever seen. It was made of soft black velvet. The dress was strapless and had a wraparound skirt, with a slit that came up to the knee.

She pulled the hanger from its hook, wondering how he'd had time to purchase the dress and hide it in here for her. Micah had taken the day off and had spent almost every minute with her. It had been an unbelievably romantic day, full of long talks and comfortable silences. Each time Paige looked into Micah's swirling blue eyes, she felt as if she knew a little bit more of his soul and he knew a little bit more of hers.

She'd been crazy to ever doubt him.

"This is perfect," Paige breathed as she held the gown up to her chest and caught her reflection in the mirror. She looked like a modern-day princess.

Giddy with anticipation, she quickly undressed and slipped into the gown. A thrill ran over her skin the moment the fabric touched her body. She twisted her hair up and pinned it back, then smiled at her reflection.

There was something magical about this night. She could feel it.

When she bent to step into her shoes, she noticed that the lining of the dress was a deep, lustrous blue silk. Paige executed a little turn, watching herself in the mirror. Whenever she moved, there was a little flash of blue that brought the attention straight to her legs. "Guess we know which part of the body Micah's into," Paige said with a little laugh.

She lifted the lid from Micah's latest care package and spritzed on a bit of the perfume she found inside. Then she opened a small velvet box and her breath caught in her throat. Inside were the most beautiful, sparkling pair of diamond earrings she'd ever seen. Hands trembling, Paige managed somehow to put them on. Then she took a step back and allowed herself one more long look in the mirror. "Perfect," she said. "Everything is going to be perfect."

Suddenly, a little surge of fear welled up in her heart, and Paige fought it back, confused. What did she have to be afraid of? Micah loved her. He'd brought her all these beautiful things. He was taking care of her. She had nothing to fear from him.

She lifted her chin, defying her own thoughts, and walked out the door into the cool evening air. It was a silent, star-filled night, and Paige let the atmosphere wash over her as she crossed the garden to the opening in the hedge on the other side. When she walked into the flower garden, she knew for sure she was living a fairy tale.

There were candles everywhere. They were strung from the tops of the hedges in Chinese lanterns, crisscrossing the sky over head. They lined the ground in small glass votives, twinkling in the light breeze. They adorned the table that was set with flawless white china and crystal. But none of the beautiful decorations could compare to the sight of Micah himself.

He was standing in the center of the garden, his eyes glowing with wonder as he gazed at her. Dressed in a black tuxedo and white tie, he looked every bit the romantic hero. And when a classical waltz began to play, filling the air all around them, he held out his arm to her. "Do me the honor?" he asked with a smile.

Paige walked over to him ever so slowly, letting him take in the full effect of the beautiful things he'd given her, then touched her fingers to his. "It would be my pleasure," she said with a slow smile.

Micah took her in his strong arms, and together they began to dance under the stars. Paige had never waltzed before, but somehow her feet knew what to do. She didn't even have to think. She looked up at Micah as they whirled around the garden, feeling dizzy. But dizzy in a way that she relished. This was the way Micah made her feel. This was the way she *should* feel about a man as wonderful as he was.

He's not a man, a little voice inside her mind cried out. *He's a demon, Paige, remember? Remember what he told you about his destiny. About the children . . .*

But Paige easily pushed that voice aside, ignoring its bizarre nonsequitors. It didn't matter that Micah was a demon. He was also a man. He'd spent his whole life doing good. The only involvement he'd had with children was improving their lives. His only destiny was to make the world a better place—and to make her feel like she'd never felt before.

Paige locked eyes with Micah as they danced, letting her body go. Letting him lead her. She couldn't tear her gaze away from the beautiful, swirling depths of his blue eyes. They drew her in. The dizziness intensified. Suddenly, all she wanted to do was to love him. To have him love her.

No, Paige! the voice cried out. *This isn't right.*

But Paige was gone. She was lost. She was falling deeper and deeper into those eyes. And she knew she didn't ever want to stop falling.

The moment Piper materialized outside the garden wall, she let go of Leo, dropped to her knees, and pressed her face as close to the peep-hole as the laws of physics would allow. It was almost impossible to focus through the fuzzy light cast by about a million candles inside the walls, but the moment she heard the music, she realized that the figures moving in the center of the garden were dancing. As the picture became clearer and clearer, Piper didn't want to believe what she was seeing. But she couldn't deny it. It was right there in front of her. "Leo," she said, her voice strained.

"What is it?" he asked, crouching down next to her.

"It's Paige and Micah," she said, blindly reaching out a hand to him until he grabbed it up in his own. "They're dancing and—"

She couldn't finish the sentence. Doing so would make the nightmare all too real. Paige was gazing up at Micah adoringly as they waltzed, and Piper recognized the dazed look on her sister's face. It was love. Pure, unadulterated love.

"We have to get in there," she said, standing again and looking up at the sky. "Where are they?"

Cole and Phoebe appeared a few feet away, and Piper ran straight to Cole, wrapping her arm around his waist. "Let's go," she said.

"Okay, hold tight," Cole said. "I've never tried to take more than one person with me before."

Leo smiled at them reassuringly, and in a moment everything went gray, then white, and then Piper was standing in a completely different place. She opened her eyes and looked around, taking in the lush rosebushes, the flowerbeds bursting with color, the perfectly trimmed lawn. Paige and Micah holding each other, their lips about to meet . . .

"Paige! No!" Piper shouted, lurching forward. She focused all the power in her body at her hands and froze the garden. Micah was suspended in time, his lips puckered, his eyes half closed, looking almost comical in the moonlight.

Paige blinked and turned to her sisters. "What did you do that for?" she asked, crossing her arms over her chest.

"See what I mean?" Piper said to Phoebe. "Where's the, 'Oh, thank God you're here?'"

Phoebe ran over to Paige and pulled her away from the frozen Micah, clutching both her wrists. "Paige, listen to me," she said, inching Paige closer to Cole and Piper. "Cole brought us here so that we could vanquish Vandalus. We have to get rid of Micah and get you the heck out of here."

Paige's face slowly screwed up into a confused frown. "Get rid of Micah?" she asked, pulling her head back slightly. She glanced at Piper as if she was baffled by Phoebe and hoping for some support. "Why would I want to get rid of him? I love him more than anything else in the world."

Piper felt any hope she had left start to wane. Paige was one of the strongest-willed people she knew. Plus she had the added benefit of being one of the Charmed Ones. If Micah could mess with her this much, what would happen if his inner demon was unleashed on an unsuspecting world?

"Paige, you have to snap out of it," Piper said firmly, reaching out and tucking a stray hair behind her sister's ear. "Micah is keeping you prisoner here, remember? He's one of the bad guys."

"One of the worst," Cole put in.

Paige's eyes flashed with anger. "You're one to talk," she spat at Cole. "At least Micah has spent his whole life helping people. What did you ever do before Phoebe came along? Besides kill innocents, I mean."

Phoebe sucked in an audible breath as Cole looked away, clearly stung. "Paige—"

"No, I don't want to hear it," Paige said, taking a few steps away from them. "I love Micah and I am going to be with him. Now, Piper, would you mind unfreezing my boyfriend?"

Piper threw her hands up and turned away from Paige. It was a lost cause. Any second, Micah was going to unfreeze naturally and catch them all here. And they had no chance of vanquishing such a powerful demon without the Power of Three.

"What do we do, Piper?" Phoebe asked, backing away slightly as Micah snapped out of it and realized Paige was no longer waiting for his kiss.

Piper grabbed Phoebe's hand, her heart pounding. "I'd say run for cover."

Chapter

14

"How?!" Micah shouted, his face contorting with rage as he whirled on Piper, Phoebe, and Cole. "How did you get in here?"

Phoebe groped the air behind her until she found Cole's hand and clutched him tightly. She wasn't about to answer the psycho demon's question and risk him attacking her boyfriend. Piper took a step in front of Cole as well, and Phoebe felt buoyed by her sister's unwavering determination and strength. Together they could fight anything. Of course having a plan B and Paige by their sides would have helped a bit.

Suddenly, she realized she was still holding the vanquishing spell and she quickly tucked it into the back pocket of her jeans. They weren't going to be able to use it until they won Paige over, so she had to keep it safe until then.

"Actually, I don't care how you got in,"

Micah said with an evil sneer, lifting his arm toward them like a weapon. "Having you all here at the same time will make this so much easier."

"Piper . . . ," Phoebe said warily, suddenly recalling the drawing of Vandalus in *The Book of Shadows*—the one that pictured him with some sort of beam emanating from his wrist.

"Scatter!" Piper shouted.

Phoebe flung herself to the ground, executing a somersault and landing crouched but on her feet, ready to strike. She felt a flash of heat sizzle past her cheek. Glancing wildly over her shoulder, Phoebe saw that Micah had somehow managed to vaporize a stone bench and burn a hole through his hedge, but Cole and Piper were still in one piece.

Phoebe struggled to catch her breath and accept the fact that Micah had yet another weapon to use against them. How were they supposed to fight this thing?

"This is the guy you love, Paige?" Piper shouted, pushing herself up from the ground.

Paige said nothing, but her face registered confusion as she looked around at the scene. If Phoebe didn't know better, she'd say her sister had never seen a demon in action before. Micah raised his arm again, his mouth twisted into a sickeningly satisfied smile, but before he could generate another blast, Cole stood and hurled a red, glowing energy ball right at Micah's chest.

"No!" Paige screamed at the top of her lungs, bringing her hands to her face as Micah was flung back several yards into the hedge at the far end of the garden.

"Wasn't counting on that, was he?" Cole said, rubbing his hands together.

"Don't get cocky yet," Phoebe said. "Piper, get Paige and snap her out of it. We'll try to hold him."

As Piper pulled Paige toward a corner of the garden—away from Micah—Phoebe and Cole launched a full-on assault. Micah was just pulling himself out of the crushed and mangled bushes when Phoebe launched herself into the air, flying the last few feet and landing a brutal kick right beneath his jaw, snapping his head back. Micah tumbled back again, but this time was only down for seconds. By the time Phoebe had returned to the ground, Micah was back on his feet.

Phoebe threw a punch, which he easily ducked, but while he was down, Cole hit him with another energy ball. For a moment, Phoebe started to think that this fight would be no problem, but then she heard Cole shout her name and she whirled around, her heart in her throat.

Cole was desperately pounding his fists against the air. He pressed his hands into invisible walls all around him. Micah had imprisoned him inside an invisible box. "Let me out of here!" Cole shouted, the veins in his neck nearly popping out of his skin as he glared at Micah.

"Cole!" Phoebe shouted, running up to him with her pulse racing. "Try an energy ball!"

He pulled his arm back and flung a fiery orb at the wall, but it simply splattered in seemingly thin air, sending a wave of red light out across the invisible walls and, for a moment, defining the corners and edges of Cole's prison before disappearing entirely.

"Phoebe! Get down!" Cole shouted suddenly, his eyes wide.

Phoebe ducked without even thinking, and Cole hit the ground right next to her. Another sizzle of heat sliced over her head and hit Cole's prison. If he hadn't ducked as well, he would have been incinerated.

"All right, that's it," Phoebe said, narrowing her eyes as she turned on Micah. "You mess with my boyfriend, you mess with me,"

Phoebe flung herself into the air and swung around midflight, flattening Micah with a round-house to the jaw. When her feet touched the ground again, she landed a punch right in his gut, then backhanded him into the bushes once again. He struggled to find his balance, but Phoebe wouldn't let up. As long as she was close enough to him to punch him, he wouldn't be able to hit her with one of his wrist beams from hell.

"Paige is never going to love you!" Phoebe shouted, blocking his arm as he swung at her and going for an uppercut.

She felt a sizzle of adrenaline as the punch was about to land, but then, out of nowhere, her oxygen was cut off. Micah had her by the throat with one, extraordinarily strong hand, and was lifting her up off the ground. Phoebe's legs flailed as she struggled for breath.

"I have news for you, little girl," Micah said as he glared up at her. "She already does."

"Phoebe!" Cole shouted as Micah flung her aside. She hit the ground with a bone-shaking thud and coughed painfully as she sucked in the night air.

"I'm bored with you now," Micah said with a short laugh. "I'd do away with you, but all I need is one kiss from your sister and then I'll have the power to hurt you in ways you've never even imagined."

Phoebe managed to push herself up to her elbows as Micah straightened his jacket and started across the garden. Her heart, her head, and her soul were all pounding with fear, but she could find her voice, barely, through all the coughing.

"Piper!" Phoebe choked out. "Piper! He's coming!"

Piper broke off her stream of rationalizations to Paige the moment she heard Phoebe's weakened voice fill her ears. She frantically checked over her shoulder, and a terrified chill raced over her skin. Cole was trapped, Phoebe was down, and Micah was coming their way. Clutching Paige's arms, Piper reeled around to look at her sister. Unfortunately, the girl she saw wasn't her sister at all. Paige was in some kind of trance. Her eyes were unfocused, she had a far-off, wistful smile on her face and her body was almost limp.

"Paige, please!" Piper said, shaking her desperately as she felt Micah advancing on them. "Please! You have to remember who you are! You're a Charmed One! Fighting evil is your destiny, and I swear to you, Micah is evil."

"I love him, Piper," Paige said dreamily, looking off past Piper's shoulder at the demon in Prince Charming clothing. "You can't fight true love."

Piper heard Micah's footsteps crunch to a stop behind her. "Give up yet, witch?" he asked in a throaty voice.

"Not quite," Piper said, setting her jaw as she turned to Micah, shielding Paige from him.

"I have to admire your determination," Micah said, tugging nonchalantly on the ends of his sleeves. Then he looked up at her and raised his eyebrows. "Oh, wait. No, I don't."

Before Piper could blink, Micah had reached out one hand and shoved her to the ground. Her face hit dirt, and the taste of it filled her mouth. He stepped over her prone body and pulled Paige to him. Piper flipped over onto her back and narrowed her eyes, focusing all her hatred for him, all the anger she'd felt over the past few days, into her power. She flung her hands out at him, expecting to blow him straight back to where he belonged.

Nothing happened.

"Nice try," Micah said, never tearing his eyes from Paige's face. He slipped his hand behind her head and pulled her toward him as she looked up into his eyes, elated.

"Damn it!" Piper shouted. She flung her hands out again and froze him once more, just seconds before his lips touched Paige's.

"Would you stop doing that!" Paige said through her teeth, rolling her eyes as if Piper were simply being a nuisance.

"Phoebe! Get your butt over here!" Piper shouted as she scrambled to her feet.

"I am," Phoebe said, appearing at Piper's side. She was a little dirty and a tad out of breath, but looked no worse for the wear.

"I can't figure out how to snap her out of this," Piper said, lifting her hand weakly in Paige's direction. She was leaning up against Micah's unmoving chest, her head tilted dreamily as she looked up at his face. "She's like a love zombie."

"Let me try," Phoebe said. She walked over to Paige and tried to pull her gently away from Micah, but Paige started to struggle.

"Why are you doing this to us?" Paige cried, trying in vain to free her wrist from Phoebe's strong grasp. "Phoebe! Let go of me!"

Paige yanked her hand so hard, Phoebe had to let go. Piper watched as angry tears filled Paige's eyes. She grasped her wrist and seemed to shrink in upon herself.

"I don't understand why you don't want me to be happy," Paige said, her voice pleading. "You don't care about me anymore. You don't let me do anything or have any of the things I want. Well, I'm here to tell you that you don't have to be burdened with me anymore. I'm going to stay here with Micah."

Piper's chest felt as if it were breaking open. She knew, on some level, that this was just the spell talking, but it was hard to watch her sister in so much pain. It was even harder to know that Paige thought she and Phoebe had caused it. "Paige, you can't mean that," she said. "You know we care about you."

"We always have and we always will," Phoebe said sincerely.

"You don't have to lie to me anymore," Paige said with a sad smile. She looked over at Micah lovingly. "Micah is a great man. He'll take care of me."

As Paige walked back over to the love of her alternate-reality life, Piper managed to tear her attention away from her heartache long enough to refocus on the task at hand. "I can't believe this," she said to Phoebe under her breath. "How are we supposed to make her see him for what he really is?"

Suddenly, Phoebe's entire face lit up and she hugged Piper in the tightest, fastest hug she'd ever experienced. "Piper! That's it!" she exclaimed before pulling back. "We can do a revelation spell!"

Piper blinked, feeling a new surge of hope well up inside of her. "Do you think it'll work?"

"If it doesn't, nothing will. You saw what that thing looked like in *The Book of Shadows*," Phoebe said, casting a disturbed glance at Micah. "If there's any Paige left in Paige, she'll wake up when she sees Vandalus."

"Okay, let's try it," Piper said. "I'll unfreeze, him and then we'll have to recite it as fast as possible—before he can kiss her."

"Here. Let's get her away from him first," Phoebe said, walking over to Paige. "That'll give us more time."

She took hold of Paige's arms again and pulled her away from the statue that was Micah.

"Phoebe! God! What are you guys *doing*?" Paige cried, struggling the whole way.

Phoebe rolled her eyes at Piper as she held Paige next to them. "Okay," she said. "Go for it."

Holding her breath, Piper raised her hands and unfroze Micah, then clutched hands with Phoebe. Micah looked around, obviously confused that Paige was no longer in his arms, then turned on the sisters. "I'm done playing now," he said, narrowing his eyes as he stalked toward Paige.

"Now!" Piper shouted. Then she and Phoebe recited the revelation spell together:

> "Mirror of life, mirror so sure,
> In your reflection all is pure.
> Behind your glass let nothing hide.
> Reveal the truth that lurks inside!"

Paige's heart seemed to be jumping rope inside her chest as Micah approached her, his magical, deep blue eyes full of pure adoration. Her skin tingled as he touched her, her mind swam as he pulled her to him. She tilted her head back, and her eyes started to close. She couldn't wait for his kiss. It seemed like forever since she'd felt it.

Then, suddenly, Micah let out a painful groan, and Paige's eyes flew open in fear. He was in pain. She had to help him

But the moment she saw Micah, she fell back, horrified. Something was happening to him. His hands clutched at his face as his head shook so violently, it seemed as if at any second it would explode. Then, as she watched, it was as if his skin had melted away, leaving behind a face so demonic, she could barely stand to look. There were a million fangs where its mouth should be, its skin was as wrinkled as a prune past its prime, and its eyes were blacker than coal.

His blue eyes. What happened to his mesmerizing blue eyes?

Suddenly, Paige felt as if she'd been shaken out of a dream. She reached out to steady herself, and her hands hit something soft. She looked left and saw Piper holding her up, then she felt Phoebe's arms wrap around her back to support her.

"You okay?" Phoebe asked, her voice hopeful.

"I think so," Paige said. Her mind was a mess of mushy, muddled, confusing thoughts, and her heart was pounding like she'd just run a 10K. But one thing was clear: There was some kind of awful demon standing where Micah had just been, and it was not happy. "What *is* that thing?" Paige asked, grimacing.

"She's back, ladies and gentlemen!" Piper said.

"Uh . . . spell time," Phoebe called out, pulling a wrinkled piece of paper out of her back pocket.

The Micah thing was barreling toward Paige and her sisters. She was still confused and foggy, but she knew she didn't want the demon to get hold of them. When Phoebe held out the spell in front of her, she recited it without giving it a second thought.

> "By the Power of Three, his spells be done,
> His evil through, his mask unspun,
> Take this monster away from us.
> Let our words vanquish Vandalus!"

• • •

Paige clung to her sisters as Vandalus's head suddenly snapped back and his arms flew up into the air. A blinding beam of red light blasted forth from each of his wrists into the night sky, and he screamed out in unearthly pain. The beams slowly widened until they met and shrouded him, and then in a blink, they were gone and Vandalus was gone with them.

"I need to sit," Paige said as her knees went out from under her.

Piper and Phoebe helped her over to a bench, and as she lowered herself down, the events of the past few days came rushing back to her in a frenzy of images. Her first night in the garden, her first starved, petrified day. But the more recent moments were the hardest to recall. She looked down at her lap and the velvet dress she'd so happily donned just a little while ago. Why had she been so happy? What had possessed her to put these things on? "Omigod, you guys," Paige said. "He was going to use the kids . . . all the kids from his orphanages and the halfway house. He said they were going to be his army."

Piper looked at Phoebe, her skin pale. "We were right. He was probably brainwashing them all along—preparing them so he'd have followers when he was finally set free in demon form."

"Brainwashing?" Paige repeated, looking up at her sisters.

"That's what he was doing to you," Phoebe explained gently. "He had you under some kind of spell."

Slowly, Paige looked around the garden. The candles were still twinkling all around her and the flowers were as beautiful as ever. She and Micah had taken such a lovely walk here just that morning and she'd felt so . . . content. And it was all a lie. A spell. Or was it? Micah's love for her had felt so real.

Suddenly, Leo materialized in front of her, and Cole stepped up behind Phoebe. Seeing them here in Micah's garden seemed so very wrong. This place belonged to her and Micah. But Micah was gone. Micah was evil.

"The force field is down," Leo said, crouching to the ground at Paige's feet and looking up into her face. "Are you all right? Is everyone all right?" he added, looking around at Piper, Phoebe, and Cole.

"We're fine—right, Paige?" Piper said, reaching out and running her hand down Paige's cheek.

"I don't know," Paige said, her eyes suddenly welling up with tears. "I don't know what happened or where I've *been* . . ." She looked up at her sisters sorrowfully. "Was that demon really Micah?" she asked, a single tear spilling over onto her cheek. "Did we just kill him?"

Piper and Phoebe exchanged a wary look before Phoebe answered. "We did, but there really was no Micah, sweetie," she said. "It was just a disguise Vandalus made up for himself."

"Oh," Paige said, looking down at her hands. She knew that. She did. But if she knew Micah was bad, then why was she so upset? Was this all part of the spell he'd cast on her?

Was she ever going to be able to discern reality from the spell again?

Exhausted and confused, Paige bent at the waist and started to cry. She barely even felt it when Leo wrapped his arms around her and orbed her out of the garden and back into her bedroom.

"Try to get some sleep," Leo said as she lay back on her soft pillows. "It's going to be okay."

Paige turned onto her side and pulled the cozy blankets up to her chin. But as relieved as she was to be in her own bed again, she couldn't seem to make herself believe Leo's words. Paige had lost her chance at love. She felt as if nothing was ever going to be okay again.

Chapter

15

Piper opened her eyes the following morning to find Leo wide awake and lying next to her, studying her face. He smiled when he saw her and she rolled over to face him, trying to hang on to the pleasant, groggy sensation left over from the small amount of sleep she'd had.

"How long have you been watching me?" she asked, stretching her arm above her head and resting her cheek on her bicep.

"Since you fell asleep," he replied, his blue eyes serious.

"And when was that?" Piper asked, her brow furrowing.

"About an hour ago," he replied. "I guess everything that happened yesterday didn't make for the greatest sleep."

Piper turned her head and looked up at the ceiling, which was dimly lit by the early morn-

ing sun. She'd lain awake for hours the night
before, going over everything that had been said
and done the past few days. Of all the horrifying things that had occurred, one theme clung
to her mind more fiercely than any other: Paige
saying that Piper and Phoebe didn't care about
her. It had come up more than once. And not
always when Paige was completely high on
Micah.

"I have to see if she's okay," Piper said, fling-
ing aside the blankets and swinging her legs
over the side of the bed.

She pushed her feet into her slippers and
padded out into the hallway, followed closely by
her husband. The moment she looked down the
hall, she paused. Phoebe and Cole were already
hovering outside Paige's bedroom door.

"I don't think she's awake yet," Phoebe whispered as Piper and Leo approached. She tilted
her ear to the door and looked at Piper, shaking
her head. "Nothing."

Piper sighed and looked at the closed door,
wishing the ability to look through walls were
one of her powers. Had Paige lain awake all
night as well? Was she in there at this very
moment, sitting on her bed, mentally cursing her
sisters for having made her kill the guy she'd
loved?

"Do you think she meant it?" Piper asked,
glancing at Phoebe.

"That stuff about us not caring about her?"

Phoebe asked, scrunching her face up. "About not letting her do anything . . . ?"

"Yeah. So you've been thinking about it, too, huh?" Piper asked, actually feeling a bit better that she wasn't the only one obsessing.

"Don't do that to yourselves," Leo said, wrapping his arms around Piper from behind and resting his chin on her shoulder. "You know Paige loves you, and she knows you love her."

"She was under Vandalus's spell," Cole put in. "It wasn't her talking."

Piper caught Phoebe's eyes and read the truth there—saw her own thoughts reflected in her sister. They both knew that Paige had been feeling slighted long before she'd ever met Micah. She'd hated their ribbing about her sugar habit; she was upset over not being allowed to use the SUV; and then there was the thing at the picnic, and the newspaper fiasco. Small incidents, but they added up. Add all that to the fact that Paige had only recently entered their lives, and Piper knew that her sister had to be feeling less than sure of her place in the family.

"I have an idea," Phoebe said suddenly.

Her face lit up with a mischievous grin, and Piper felt a little sizzle of excitement skitter through her. When Phoebe smiled like that, it usually meant she had something seriously fun up her sleeve.

"Do tell," Piper said. She linked her arm with Phoebe's and pulled her off down the hallway, leaving their men behind them, shaking their heads.

Paige pulled her brush through her hair absently, standing in front of the mirror but gazing past her reflection. Her body felt as if it had been knocked around by a world-class fighter, and her brain hadn't faired much better. Although matters were much more clear this morning, she still couldn't help feeling depressed over everything that had happened.

A few days ago, she'd been supremely happy, thinking she'd found an amazing guy. And now it had all been ripped away from her in the most horrifying way possible.

She heaved a sigh and placed her brush down on top of her dresser. As she turned toward the door, the black velvet dress she'd woken up in caught her eye. It was strewn on her wicker chair in the corner, rumpled and ruined—the last vestige of her fairy-tale life.

Paige shook her head at herself, reached out her hand, and said, "Dress." The gown orbed into her palm, and she rolled it up in a ball and stuffed it into her garbage can. "So much for dreams coming true," she said morosely. Then she picked up the small garbage can and hugged it to her chest as she walked out of her room and down the stairs.

When she reached the first floor, she started for the door, intending to get rid of the dress right away, but her hand froze on the doorknob.

That smell . . . could it be?

Still hugging the garbage can, Paige walked into the kitchen, hearing the clanging and clanking of pots and pans well before she arrived. Piper was serving up chocolate-chip pancakes, eggs, and muffins while Phoebe was laying out a sheaf of newspapers on the table. Neither of them had noticed Paige's entrance.

"What're you guys doing?" Paige asked slowly as she placed the garbage can on the floor.

Her sisters both looked up and shouted in unison, "Surprise!" Paige felt a smile tug at the corners of her mouth. No small feat considering a few minutes ago she was thinking about never smiling again. "Is this all for me?" she asked, walking over to the table and taking in the spread.

Not only were the platters that covered the table heaped with all her favorite breakfast foods, but the entertainment sections from four newspapers were lying next to her plate. Phoebe leaned in to the back of one of the chairs, watching Paige's reaction.

"You guys didn't have to do this," Paige said, her face nevertheless growing pink with pleasure.

"We know," Piper said, walking up next to Phoebe. "But we wanted to apologize for being so scatterbrained lately."

"The thing is, we're always scatterbrained,"

Phoebe said with a chuckle. "You have to try not to take it personally, because if we forget stuff, it doesn't mean we don't care about you."

"But we *are* going to try not to forget so much," Piper put in.

"And we are going to give you this," Phoebe added. She walked over to the counter next to the sink and picked up a little red box, which she brought over to Paige, handing it to her ceremoniously.

"What is it?" Paige asked, eyeing her sisters.

"You won't know unless you open it," Piper said, crossing her arms over the front of her navy blue sweater.

Paige lifted the top off the box, expecting from its size to find some kind of jewelry. But what she saw inside made her heart skip a beat. She put one finger inside the box and lifted out the prettiest ring she'd ever seen.

A *key* ring. With actual keys on it.

"Are these what I think they are?" Paige asked, her eyebrows shooting up.

"Keys to the SUV," Piper said with a nod. "Just . . . be careful."

"Piper!" Phoebe protested.

"Sorry!" Piper said with a laugh. "We should have given them to you a long time ago," she told Paige.

"Thanks, you guys," Paige said, touched.

Piper wrapped her arms around her, and Paige hugged her back, squeezing her eyes shut.

Then Phoebe joined in, circling her arms around both of them.

"We're just glad to have you back," Phoebe said.

"I'm glad to be back," Paige said sincerely.

When she finally pulled away, Paige took a step back and leaned against the island in the center of the kitchen. She looked down at the key ring, twisting it around and around her finger. "I want you guys to know that I'm sorry," Paige said slowly, keeping her eyes downcast. "I'm sorry I got myself captured and I'm sorry I was such an idiot last night."

"It's okay," Piper said, reaching out to rub Paige's arm comfortingly. "We know you weren't yourself."

"Yeah, but I have no excuse for not listening to you earlier in the week," Paige said, finally managing to pull her eyes away from the keys to look at her sisters. She felt so dumb, so naive, so chagrined. How could they ever respect her after how irrational she'd been?

"But I want you guys to know this whole thing has taught me a few good lessons," she said seriously. She took a deep breath. "First, I'm always going to listen to your warnings. I'm not saying I'm always going to follow them, because I have my own mind, but I'll definitely consider them for a tad longer than zero seconds."

Phoebe and Piper both laughed, and Paige couldn't help smiling as well.

"Number two, I am not going to rush head-first into a relationship just because I want one," Paige continued, a lump forming in her throat as she thought of the pre-demon Micah. "Just call me Caution Girl from now on."

"I thought *you* were Caution Girl," Phoebe said to Piper with mock seriousness.

"She can borrow the moniker for a while," Piper shot back.

Paige pushed herself away from the counter and pulled out her chair, ready to get down to the culinary task at hand.

"What's number three?" Phoebe asked as she dropped into the chair to Paige's left.

"Huh?" Paige asked.

"Number three? You said a *few* good lessons, and a few is more than two, so what's number three?" Phoebe prompted.

"Oh," Paige said, turning beet red as she lowered herself into her chair. "Number three is I definitely don't want a demon boyfriend—no offense, Phoebe."

Phoebe just looked at her for a second, and Paige was certain her sister was going to throw a fit, but then Phoebe burst out laughing. "None taken," Phoebe said, grabbing a muffin out of the basket in the center of the table.

"Let's eat!" Piper called out as she brought the orange juice pitcher over and sat down as well.

Paige smiled happily as she served herself a

stack of pancakes and her sisters started to chat about the upcoming performers at P3. She knew she wasn't going to be ready to date again for a long, *long* time. But eventually, Paige knew she was going to find her true love.

And in the meantime, she had the love of two Charmed sisters.

About the Author

Emma Harrison is an editor-turned-writer who has worked on many series, including Sweet Valley High Senior Year, Roswell High, and Fearless. She never misses an episode of *Charmed*.

DATE WITH
DEATH

As Piper and Leo contemplate parenthood and Phoebe
and Cole enjoy their engagement, Paige is feeling more of
a push to find a significant other. In a moment of whimsy,
she signs up for an online dating service. Needless to say,
she soon finds herself flooded with eager responses.
Almost every night she embarks on a new date that seems
to lead nowhere – despite the fact that Paige has a
perfectly good time when she's out.

Or does she? Before long, the sisters discover that Paige
spends her "dates" in a catatonic trance – she hasn't actually
gone anywhere! Soon afterward, her suitors are discovered
to have committed evil acts. Paige is acting as a conduit for
dark powers – and soon she is projecting her energies onto
her sisters. Will Piper and Phoebe be able to save her
using only the Power of Two?